Praise for story collections by V.S. Kemanis

"Rich in metaphors and intensely provocative descriptive passages, these stories are to be tasted, savored, enjoyed and read over and over again. *Your Pick: Selected Stories* is a powerful tribute to this author's mastery of the art of creating not just a good story, but a story that needs to be read many times to appreciate the full power of its presentation." — *Readers' Favorite*

"Eleven compulsively readable short stories... Anyone who appreciates supple writing and fine storytelling will enjoy every minute spent reading these stories... A good deal of the pleasure in the collection comes from the writing itself. Kemanis knows how to build a story and keep it going." — *Foreword Reviews* on *Love and Crime: Stories*

"[Kemanis is] unarguably gifted...a great talent... There are stories here that I think I will remember forever. They've stayed with me in the weeks since I read them and make me smile even now as I call to mind their wonderfully flawed characters, their gentle humor, their twists and surprises and, without exception, the compassionate insight at their core." — *SP Reviews* on *Dust of the Universe*

"V. S. Kemanis is certainly one of the most intelligent writers I have read, writers of classics included. Her insight into human behavior is truly unusual... These are believable stories and believable characters... Unwaveringly fascinating." — *The Kindle Book Review* on *Everyone But Us*

"Quietly effective... Perfectly paced and brimming with mood and insight into our darker moments... Kemanis pulls off the difficult trick of imbuing the humdrum with a subliminal disquiet." — David Antrobus, author of *Dissolute Kinship,* on *Malocclusion*

Malocclusion
tales of misdemeanor

V.S. Kemanis

Copyright © 2013 V.S. Kemanis
2022 edition

The following stories were originally published in slightly different form in these literary journals: *Lynx Eye*: "Cat"; *Thema*: "Significant Details"; and in these print collections by the author: *Women I've Known, Stories*: "Times Square Tail," "Road," "Significant Details," "Quicker Forms of Death," "To Fly," "Between Boys and Men," "A Simple Case"; and *Gray Zone, Stories*: "Cat," "The Piano Teacher's Lover," and "Gray Zone."

Malocclusion, tales of misdemeanor
B&P Readers' Choice Awards Nominee 2014

ISBN-13: 978-0-9965909-0-7
ISBN-10: 0-9965909-0-0

℞ **Opus Nine Books**
•**New York**•

For Kevin, with love

CONTENTS

∼CAT

KAREN PONDERED THE AFTERMATH. Angelic in death, Cloud lay silent, pristine white, legs extended straight down in two, perfect inverted Vs. Perhaps not dead, but on further look, yes, certainly so. Motionless, at rest, a tiny trickle of blood from the side of the mouth, the fatal injuries—broken bones, punctured organs—all internal and mercifully hidden from view by that silky cumulous thickness.

Gazing upon the animal in the falling light, Karen felt empty of emotion, suspicious only of incipient dread. Something was going to happen to her because of this, an irreversible something hidden under that voice in her head, a rational, pallid monotone: *The cat is dead. You have killed the cat. But it was an accident that couldn't be helped.*

She looked up to her right at the mouth of Jaclyn Temple's long driveway. Further in, shielded from view by a jungle of overgrowth, stood the contemporary redwood home. Private, secluded. Jaclyn couldn't have witnessed her cat's death. Karen glanced to her left at the Overmeyers' house across the street, then at the Brewsters' next door. Quiet. Dusk. Families at their dinner tables, unaware. At the end of the cul-de-sac, Ben and the twins would be awaiting Karen's return from a quick trip to the market, bringing milk for dinner.

She stood and leaned against the hood of her car, allowing her eyes to fall on the cat once again. No, she wouldn't lift it; she could imagine the feel of those soft-jelly insides beneath the thick coat, and perhaps there was blood matting up underneath, absorbed by the fur. A rhythmic clicking was the only sound, marking the pulse of orange light from the Peugeot, her steady and safe chariot. Apparently, quite automatically, Karen had applied the brake, turned off the engine and hit the hazard light button, although she had no memory of these actions.

Parallel lines of sparkling dots blinked on, outlining the perimeter of the Temples' driveway like a smuggler's runway snaked into the trees. Beckoned, Karen side-stepped Cloud and traversed the runway until she stood at Jaclyn's threshold, facing that large etched-in-oak WELCOME sign hanging by a chain on the front door under a bright, halogen lamp.

Despite the lights and the WELCOME, Jaclyn's door oddly lacked a bell. Beneath the sign jutted an old-fashioned brass knocker that, Karen had always suspected, required the use of considerable force to elicit a response from within. To be heard and seen by Jaclyn took effort, an effort that Karen had expended on many occasions with objectively satisfactory results, Jaclyn's response always appropriate, defying any real need for complaint.

She hesitated, lifted the knocker high and aided its

fall. In the twenty seconds before Jaclyn came to the door, Karen's mind opened to a picture of that first day, now over a year ago. She'd waited a decent amount of time, a week after the moving trucks had come and gone, before baking a zucchini-nut loaf and arriving at the Temples' doorstep, bread still warm inside the foil wrapper. The WELCOME sign, recently hung, was coincidentally positioned within a spot of sunshine, burning down into the clearing shaved from the woods for the house.

As the door opened, the sign swung out from its chain and gave a wooden clunk at the moment her new neighbor appeared, wearing an earth-toned caftan, tall and striking, her black hair pulled into a French bun with a single line of natural white growing from the temple, dipping down at the side, ending inside the knot in back. The white streak suggested a wisp of Cloud, cradled snuggly, slit-eyed and purring, in the crook of her owner's left arm. Jaclyn smiled softly with raised eyebrows at Karen's welcome-committee "hello," her right hand floating up without thought to the arched mound of white fur, as if she were stroking her own arm or neck.

This time, of course, Jaclyn appeared at the door catless and alone. She had a husband, but Mr. Temple was rarely seen, no more than a shadowy figure at the wheel of a new Lexus, emerging from that driveway early in the morning. Always, for every neighborly sort of contact, Jaclyn and Cloud had been the Temple family representatives.

Karen said nothing immediately, suddenly panicky, wondering at her involuntary need for exposure. After all, she could have driven away and no one would have been the wiser.

"Hello," said Jaclyn with a sort of smile-frown, something appropriate for an unannounced visit at the dinner hour.

Karen screwed up her courage. Nothing to do but say it straight out. "There's been an accident."

Jaclyn's brow wrinkled, her eyes searching for obvious injuries. "Are you all right?"

"Well, yes." Too late. Perhaps a "no" would have been better. "I'm not hurt, that is. But, I'm so sorry, your cat…"

The wrinkle deepened. Her face remained unchanged except for the furrowed brow that said everything. "Where is she now?" Jaclyn looked beyond Karen's shoulder into the driveway, as if Cloud might be limping home.

"Out…" Karen motioned toward the road. "I didn't know whether to lift her. I'm so sorry, but she just *darted* into the street."

Jaclyn's dark eyes shifted slowly onto Karen and stopped there. She suspected the worst, Karen could tell. There was nothing more to say. In silence, the women turned from the door and marched out the driveway, Karen two steps ahead with her arms crossed tightly, holding her insides rigid and protected from Jaclyn's cool exterior, pressing in at her back.

Night had now fallen, allowing the hazard lights to define fleeting orange outlines of trees in blackness, each flash ticking off another second between here and there, the moments remaining before the full impact of Jaclyn's grief and Karen's plummet.

As they emerged from the driveway, Jaclyn at once spotted Cloud's white glowing mass, eerily more visible than it had been at dusk. Stepping around Karen with long, intent strides, she came up to the animal's side, crouched, felt here and there, gingerly. She touched the cat's neck, ran a finger along the pads of one paw, stroked the body, lifted the tip of the tail and laid it to rest, placed a finger under the nose, cupped and cradled the head. After she'd done all these things, she fell heavily from her squat onto the side of her right thigh and placed a hand on Cloud's abdomen. "Already cold," she said.

"I'm so sorry," said Karen, more for herself than for Jaclyn.

After the delivery of the nut loaf, there'd been a few coincidental meetings and pleasant chats at the entrance to Jaclyn's driveway, once when Karen stopped to lean out her car window, the second time as she walked her eight-year-olds back from the school bus stop. Each time, Cloud sat snuggly in the crook of her owner's arm while Jaclyn completed her task with the free hand: setting out the newspapers for recycling or retrieving mail from the mailbox.

Karen's twins, Devon and Kimberly, fell immediately in love with Cloud. In the way of young children, spontaneous and uninhibited, they ran up to Jaclyn without hesitation or introduction, yet mindful of their mother's lessons on manners, asking "Please, please," could they pet the beautiful cat? Jaclyn smiled warmly while delivering a caveat along with her assent: "Yes, but

I'm afraid that Cloud is somewhat wary of strangers."

An odd way to put it, thought Karen as she watched Devon slowly reaching up with amazing self-restraint against her eagerness, *little children and neighbors at that*, inching closer to the silky mound of fur while Kimmy patiently waited her turn, *"somewhat wary of strangers,"* extending her fingertips and touching gently, when suddenly a "hsss!" and a darting claw! Little Devon's face crumpled with disappointment. "She doesn't like me!" exclaimed the girl. Karen lifted her daughter's hand, found the raised pink streak and asked, "Are you hurt?" Between the two of them—and only the mother of such *identical* twins would know this—Devon was the more sensitive and least likely to rebound from an assault. And although Jaclyn's face was filled with compassion, she did not apologize. After all, her eyes seemed to say, children should learn the value of a proper warning.

When Karen returned home with the milk, she said nothing to Ben and the twins, who didn't seem to notice the extra fifteen minutes she'd been gone. The girls were petty and quarrelsome, something that Karen usually wouldn't tolerate, but she remained silent. Not unpleasantly so. She was partially present at the dinner table, her eyes opened to her husband and children but seeing other things while her face maintained the placid expression of inner peace. *Even the best of us have accidents—it couldn't be helped.*

She ran a replay of Jaclyn slowly rising to her knees, bending forward to scoop up the animal, one hand under the head, another hand under the hind quarters, lifting and pressing the cat firmly against her breast, unmindful of the blood, dirt, gravel, and oil that would stain her caftan, standing awkwardly with a tiny stumble, coming to right, not seeming to notice Karen's second, or perhaps third, apology with an ineffectual, "If there's anything I can do…" Jaclyn turned away and whispered, "I'll just lay her to rest," as she drifted toward her driveway, an apparition swallowed by the trees.

Ben noticed the pictures in Karen's eyes. Later that night, when the children had gone to bed, he asked what was wrong, and she conveyed the story in a vague sort of way, which was exactly the way she remembered it.

"So, the cat just…?" he asked.

"All I know is the cat was suddenly there."

"…darted out?"

"I remember the sound. The thud. Oh, my God!"

"I'm sorry," he said. "In a way, though, it's better that you never got to know her well. Jaclyn, I mean. You never quite hit it off." Stunned, Karen looked at her husband, wondering how he could know that it mattered to her.

"But you should tell the girls. They were fond of the cat."

"I will," she said. "Tomorrow."

Despite the bad start, the girls eventually eased into a relationship with Cloud. There were days when they were playing in the neighborhood and saw Cloud at the end of the driveway, near the street. Free of her owner's protective arm, Cloud would act differently, aloof without the hostility. Standing or sitting still, she would pretend she didn't notice the children as they approached her, cautiously, hands at their sides. Once close enough, Kimmy and Devon would crouch down and coo things like, "Nice kitty," and soon, they graduated to brief and tentative touches. Depending on her mood, Cloud would bat a paw—playfully this time—or lay back and enjoy being stroked and tickled on the neck.

Karen saw some of this and knew the rest because her twins told her. Anything having to do with animals was big news and eagerly conveyed, unlike other information that required subtle forms of coercion to elicit. The children frequently asked for pets, anything from dragonflies to dogs, but ever since Jaclyn and Cloud moved in, they very clearly wanted a cat. Not just any cat. A cat with thick, long white fur. Karen delivered the standard answer: "No. I have enough animals in the house already."

To Karen's mind, children were the only kind of animal worth serious consideration. She'd wanted more of them, and there'd been the two miscarriages after the twins, and maybe she and Ben would try again, but pets instead? She'd rather devote her time to the twins, not to an animal they would abandon as soon as the novelty wore off. Her thinking on this might be different if she were older and had no children at all—if she were a person like Jaclyn. Childless by choice or cruel fate? Perhaps Karen had it wrong and there were adult Temple children somewhere, living away from home. But she suspected not. Childless women were so prominently childless, their barrenness evident in the way they smiled and talked to the children of others.

And in Jaclyn's case, one indication seemed to be her glaring lack of interest in Devon and Kimberly's identicalness. As if she simply hadn't noticed. Didn't *everyone* have something to say the first time? Karen had gotten so used to the comments and compliments that she kept a repertoire of pat responses on the tip of her tongue, always ready for quick, good-natured repartee. But Jaclyn, upon first sight of the twins, had said nothing, hadn't even done the usual double take.

Surely Jaclyn wouldn't be shy to comment the next time. Without hesitation, Karen invited her over for coffee, choosing a morning when the children would be in school, Ben at work. Jaclyn graciously accepted, and as the appointed day approached, Karen half wondered if she would arrive alone or with Cloud on her arm. So easily and naturally they would come in and sit down, those Siamese sisters—forearm glued to furry ribcage— Jaclyn lifting her coffee cup with the free hand, pinky extended, bringing the cup gently up to Cloud's lips, the sly smile and cobalt eyes, the dainty, human-like sip and a *meow, more cream please*.

But Jaclyn arrived without the cat, wearing a caftan of sky and water tones, blues and gray-greens. She stepped through the door looking doubly childless and alone, yet taller and straighter because of it, broad shouldered and confident without a hint of ill ease. Her sudden presence in the foyer, filling it up with dramatic closeness, rendered Karen momentarily speechless, something unusual. At once exotic and down-to-earth, Jaclyn possessed distinction without eccentricity and a pull that seemed to invite proximity. Especially now, standing alone, without the cat.

Karen led her guest into the kitchen where she'd laid the table with flowers and her prettiest stoneware in neat place settings amidst good coffee and cake smells, with a hope that now seemed transparent for its desire to impress with simplicity and goodness: a childlike tea party dream.

"Lovely kitchen," said Jaclyn.

"Thank you. Would you like to see the rest of the house?" Karen made the offer, knowing she would like to see every room of Jaclyn's house someday.

Jaclyn smiled. There was an evident pause before she answered, "All right, then."

Slightly rattled, Karen commenced the tour, explaining the obvious and pointing out photographs and mementos while a pleasant-faced Jaclyn followed, uttering polite assurances: "The children's room, yes," and "Ah! the dining room," and "I can see why it's your favorite; they're smiling so nicely." Ten minutes later, her life in four walls thus explained, Karen was ready for the certainty of her stoneware place settings and the secure hardness of cane-backed chairs.

Jaclyn took her coffee black and sipped slowly, ending only halfway down, remaining cool and unbent by Karen's urge to move faster. Inexplicable: her guest's perfect composure and seeming indifference to their lack of progress. Karen's usual ease with language and skill at maneuvering the S-curves of personality had all vanished beneath the banner of her desire to delve deeply and her inability to understand. At the end of an hour, she'd volunteered most of her life history and had learned little of her new neighbor's.

Jaclyn pushed back from the table. "It's been lovely, but I should get back to work."

Work? Karen was taken aback. "Oh? Where do you work?"

"At home. I travel occasionally, but most of it can be done from my desk. The wonders of telephone, email, and computer!" Jaclyn was out in the foyer by then, in transition between coffee hour and the better part of her day, unaware of her hostess's need to know and struggle with language. A question was blurted and an answer given, a complete statement of the nature of Jaclyn's employment, said in a way that betokened its every-dayness. But Karen, who'd found nothing obvious about Jaclyn, remained stuck in her own formulation of the question, unable to render meaning to the answer that followed. There was a company name and a short job description with technical sounding words.

After this, the next part was easy to interpret. "Thank you so much for the coffee," said Jaclyn, stepping onto the front walkway.

"You're welcome! Thanks for coming! We should do it again sometime."

To which Jaclyn simply smiled and waved before turning away.

The return invitation, the one that Karen expected, never came. There were more chance meetings at the end of the driveway, polite and pleasant conversation. Nothing even as intimate as Jaclyn's work was discussed, since Karen feared that her questions would be embarrassingly indicative of her ignorance or inattentiveness.

Soon after, the uninvited visits began. There were many of them, every one perfectly justifiable. A diversion up the long driveway to Jaclyn's door required a legitimate explanation, and Karen always had one, even if she sometimes stretched the limits of legitimacy, like the time she was out on a brisk walk and strode into the thicket, traversed the runway, banged the knocker hard, and asked Jaclyn with a big healthy smile if she might like to join her for the exercise. Jaclyn, wearing a caftan in muted lavender, mauve, and burgundy tones, gave Karen a tepid look and said, "Thank you, but I'm afraid I have a deadline to meet." Cloud's gaze, from the comfort of Jaclyn's arm, was equally lukewarm. Noticing the cordless phone receiver in a dangling hand, Karen apologized for the intrusion, explaining that she had tried to call but the line had been busy.

Landing, decelerating on the way out the runway, she attempted an image of Jaclyn in exercise clothes, feeling uneasy but not cognizant of mistake. The tepidness could have been only shyness.

And so there were several other attempts, Karen couldn't be sure of the number. She wasn't counting. If Jaclyn wasn't impressed with homemade cakes or well-behaved identical offspring or exercise programs, Karen would find the hook that sold. She sensed repetitiveness and rising desperation in her behavior but ignored it, wondering only vaguely at the growing uneasiness in these manufactured contacts. After all, there was nothing wrong with showing neighborly concern, like the time she warned Jaclyn about the rabid raccoon wandering the street. And it was only friendly (wasn't it?) to invite her new neighbor to join a book discussion group with friends, or out to lunch, or over (again and again) for coffee. Yet, each invitation was met with a polite refusal.

Then there were visits that could only be deemed absolutely necessary. Like the time Karen was canvassing for signatures on a petition to shut down a local nuclear facility. Jaclyn, cat on arm, signed without question. And the time she went with the twins selling Girl Scout cookies. Jaclyn and Cloud purchased three boxes in a hurry. And the last time, after Devon had recovered one of Cloud's toys, a chewable mouse, from the pachysandra near the end of the Temples' driveway. Karen assured her daughter she would return the toy, and the next day she paid a visit, unaware that it would be the last time she saw the cat alive. "So sorry to bother you," she said, now habitually prefacing her demands with excuses, "but my daughter, bless her heart, found one of Cloud's little toys, and I promised her I would return it personally, she was so sure that the cat would miss it!" Karen dangled the toy before Cloud, who regarded it noncommittally.

With her stoniest look yet, Jaclyn accepted the well-used article and said, "We have several of these, but I *do* know how important it is to honor a promise. Thank you."

Now, what did *that* mean? Further conversation was not forthcoming, and so, once again, Karen turned and walked away, without an invitation inside.

The morning after, confessions out of mind, forgetfulness was conveniently excused by the rush of daily routine.

Breakfast to eat, hair to comb, lunches to make, school backpacks to check. The girls raced out the door to the bus stop, Karen two steps behind. Kimberly challenged Devon to a skipping contest while their mother lagged, wondering at the cause of her fatigue.

But then, as they approached Jaclyn's driveway, she was struck with the horror of it: her little girls skipping so close to that spot in the road. Could there be a telltale sign, a bloodstain? It had been dark and she hadn't seen, hadn't stopped to look. "Better run!" Karen yelled at her daughters. "You're going to miss the bus!" And run they did, right past the driveway, not stopping to gather the evidence of Karen's crime. *Not a crime, but an accident that couldn't be helped.*

And, funny, Karen's quick glance on her way past yielded no obvious clues, as if nothing had happened. So convincingly normal did everything look that she put it out of mind and focused on the children again, easily catching up to them at the bus stop because, after all, they weren't so terribly late. The twins jumped into play with their friends, while Karen merely nodded a hello at their moms, feeling slightly apart despite the utter normalcy of the morning, feeling, for the first time, that she belonged to a secret, shameful society ruled by aberrant desire and behavior.

But then, just as always, that familiar yellow hulk clamored toward them and screeched to a halt with flashing red lights. "Goodbye girls! I love you!" *I do love them so much.* But the girls, caught up in their own world, barely looked her way, something that children always seemed to do when their mothers needed just the opposite.

Once the bus was off, Karen waved goodbye to the neighbor moms, these women with whom she'd shared so much. Coffee, advice, carpools, favors, children's play-dates. She'd seen the insides of their homes many times. Why wasn't it enough? "Going on my walk!" she chirped and strode off in the opposite direction. Nothing unusual, one of her brisk morning walks, a convenient façade to cover her intention of returning once they'd gone and heading straight for that spot, the source of her secret deviance, knowing she'd find it there.

On the way back, nearing Jaclyn's driveway, she moved into the center of the road where she might have stopped the Peugeot, her eyes searching the ground. Nothing, just as she'd thought, but no, out the corner of her eye she saw it, some distance away on the side of the road. No more than several inches out from the curb. A large reddish-brown splotch, the distinct color of blood. Not in the middle of the road, but close to the curb. So close. She walked up to the stain, inspected it, knew what it must be, still doubting, refusing to accept this new evidence that threatened to violate her neatly sealed protective box. She tore her eyes away and headed for home, for the comfort of ritual.

But when she returned, she could only stand silently, helplessly, in the middle of her disheveled kitchen, the single room out of order in her neat home. The breakfast dishes, the bills, the errands awaited. Yet she couldn't move and simply stood for a very long time, wishing only for relief from her anticipation, the nagging certainty she'd glimpsed the night before: something, an irreversible something, was about to happen.

The doorbell rang. Longingly, she glanced about the kitchen, at the breakfast dishes, the rose-covered tablecloth, the ruffled curtains.

The doorbell rang again.

With another aimless glance, Karen shuffled to the front door and opened it. Finally, Jaclyn had come to visit.

The stunned silence and quiet grief of the previous evening had vanished. In its place, a monstrous anger simmered under the perfect exterior, the French bun, the elegant caftan in black and gray tones. Karen remained silent, awaiting her punishment.

"I've tried to tell you in every way I know how," said Jaclyn, bold and defiant. "I didn't want a confrontation. But you refused to see things, and now you've done *this*."

This, the shameful thing, exploded with the flashes of memory of all those polite refusals, all the proper warnings. "But…I did see. I just didn't… Maybe I couldn't—"

"Accept it." Jaclyn leveled her gaze at Karen and shook her head slowly, eyes cold and accusing. She spoke distinctly, enunciating each word. "Then accept *this*. Cloud does not *dart* into the street." Jaclyn turned around, took three steps from the door, and swiveled to face Karen again for the last time. *"She never darts."*

Karen froze, grabbing at the sickness in her gut as she watched Jaclyn float away under the billowing fabric. Tears would come later, along with the futility of remorse and enlightenment—too late.

For now, the buried images beckoned and resurfaced

with the clarity of fact: Cloud stepped sedately off the curb, taking a single step, then another, head turned up, eyes shining in the headlights. Cautiously, she waited for the car to pass, remaining fixed near the curb like a white marble statue.

But then there was a pull to the right, the wheel was pulling toward the curb, and Karen's hand was guiding it...

∿TIMES SQUARE TAIL

HE PEERED INTO the shoebox, its contents layered low. *Can't avoid it much longer—need more cards.* Still a few Cameron Doughertys left, Mitchell Crawfords, Pierce Bentleys. He shook the box and gave it a short jerk upward, flipping some like flapjacks. Only one landed face up: G. Carroll Silver, Private Investigator. "P.I. Silver" plucked out the card, opened his wallet, and probed an inside slit, finding entry in front of a forgotten Crawford.

Today, Silver was working the Belle Aire all the way west on 42nd. Times Square had sucked him in years ago. As many times as he strayed—just to be safe—he always returned. The sad inhabitants fed him only indirectly, providing the attraction and camouflage for the unlikely ones, his marks, women who could easily afford the Waldorf or Plaza. Fearing detection by their own kind, they shunned their natural habitats in favor of the unsavory places more fitting to the lovers they'd carefully chosen from another world, men with little money or etiquette but skillful in the ways of the flesh.

To someone who was looking, these women were

easy to spot. Dressing down and changing neighborhoods didn't shield them from the likes of Silver. They always wore the indicators, the forgotten diamond earrings, the perfect manicure, and the little vulnerabilities that gave Silver an opening, their responses predictable. He enjoyed their faces at the moment of detection. Young or old, most of them middle-aged, each face revealed that tinge of youthful innocence sprung from guilty knowledge. The five-year-old with her hand in the cookie jar: eyes widening, complexion suddenly pale then slowly flushing with a surge of panicky thoughts. From the outside, one could never measure the ratio of embarrassment to fear, a formula determined by the secrets left at home, the indifference or brutality awaiting her there.

Silver loved every one of those faces, and he thought of them at times like these, low times when money was tight. He was in the business for himself, but he also liked to think he did it for them.

He remembered the face of the woman who'd gotten him started. Her husband—Silver's client—had been the cruel, sadistic type. Silver couldn't deliver a bad report to a man like that. But he also knew that the woman would pay if he promised secrecy. It was an easy jump to the next thought. Why deal with the husbands at all? He could still enjoy the best parts: the surveillance, the chase, and that look on their sweet faces at the moment of truth. Getting paid wasn't enough for him. He also needed their gratitude.

So, he closed his office with its unnecessary expense (giving up the steady income as well), choosing to work only for himself and for them, his women. In this way he

became their conscience, that little warning bell intervening before something worse could befall them.

But lately his luck had run dry, one bum steer setting
up another. Looks could fool. He'd wasted his time on
too many dogs who didn't need a conscience or a savior,
women who deserved where they were headed. It wasn't
his fault entirely. Bad tips, unfortunate circumstances—
nothing that reflected on his own skill. He had to believe
that.

And he had to believe today would be different. Still,
his wallet forbade extravagance. Only two hundred in
twenties left in his billfold from the six hundred he'd
made on his last good hit almost a month ago, and most
of that would be going for rent.

He saved the subway fare and walked the thirteen
blocks from his SRO in Hell's Kitchen to 42nd. Along
the way, he spied a clean copy of the *Post* near the top of
a wire-wicker trash can, picked it up, and shoved it folded
under his arm. The walk did him good, rattled the sleep
out of his head. Coffee would help, but he had to hike for
a cheap cup at a place he knew near Times Square. Thirty
cents a cup, a buttered roll for fifty.

Silver picked up his step, clamping two sides of his
collar around his neck. His best plaid sport jacket, a wool
blend, hung loosely, creating a vacuum between lining
and body that pulled up the chill October wind. The
bright sun did little to ease the bite. *Trench coat season and
not a decent one to wear, ever since that bitch dug her claws into
my neck, enough to bloody the collar.* Almost got the hair too,
but he'd saved it in time. The wind gusted; he touched the
top of his head gingerly, confirming its position, the little

mat he so carefully combed and put to bed on his dresser every night.

Standing at an open-air counter near the triangle that was the Square, Silver wolfed his roll and sipped the scalding translucent liquid down an inch as he gazed up to where the ball would soon be dropping on 1977. Tomato and cheese steam escaped the vent of a neighboring pizzeria, nauseating him. He clamped a plastic lid on the cardboard cup and took the remainder along. Only a few blocks to the Belle Aire, past the arcades, the triple X's, one or two pushers mumbling low. Twelve straight up, and only a few hookers out for the lunchtime johns. Silver usually began his workday at noon. Some of the hammers held regular jobs, dashing to the Square when the whistle blew, enough time to get some tail and make it back in an hour, sweaty but richer.

He paused outside the crumbling Aire and took in the sidewalks while sipping warmth through a hole, then turned to go inside. No one obvious yet. Tommy, massively leaning into his own *Post* behind the counter, lifted puffy lids and nodded at Silver.

"Anything yet?" asked the P.I.

Tommy grunted and shook his head, jiggling the bag of fat beneath his lips. "Slow day," he said.

"Give me something good this time."

"The last one was good."

"The last one ruined my coat."

Tommy shrugged and dropped his eyes to the paper. *Worthless piece of...* The trouble with bad times was the expense, people like Tommy. Sure, Silver could go it alone, he'd done it before, plenty. A lot of Silver's women loved to leave clues, a kind of self-sabotage: dropping credit card receipts, flashing preprinted checks, talking loudly at the hotel reception desk. The name is what got them. He had to have a name, real or phony, and he liked to think he could get it on his own, but just now he needed the help of his referral service.

Silver would never admit it, but his confidence had suffered. Bad times could get to him, swirling downward like the blood in his toothpaste, picking up soap scum and whiskers on the way into the vortex. It started with diminishing income, little doubts, little needs and little expenses eating up more income, adding more doubts, more needs, more expenses. He wasn't desperate yet, his mind still rational, carefully weighing his options. That's why he'd chosen the Belle Aire, a place as good as any other, and Tommy charged only twenty a name. But Silver would have to pay for it, even if the mark was a dud.

Silver walked to his usual corner of the lobby to set up shop in the lime-green and burgundy upholstered chair with a side table for his coffee. He sat, sending a plume of dust particles into a slender shaft of light entering through a window above Tommy's head, a window placed miraculously to catch a noontime ray between city buildings. Planting one foot snugly in a worn shoeprint of carpet, perching the other on opposite knee, he opened the *Post*, flipped the pages, and sipped.

He didn't have to wait long before she arrived. He knew her immediately.

Head down, eyes glancing up from under his oily

brow, Silver made her out. She walked in on low heels in a velveteen coat, something cheap but new, purchased for the occasion. *Always think they can blend in like that, but it's a dead giveaway*. Gleaming auburn hair, the salon color and style too perfect. Walking along Silver's horizon line from the revolving door to the reception desk, she was halting and hesitant, eyes skating the lobby.

She spotted Silver, he was sure of it, although he'd taken care not to allow his eyes to meet hers. His presence in the background was essential. He never hid but remained in plain view, available for nervous glances. Later it would help, his face remembered with a tiny jolt of shock. Yes, you were that man in the lobby.

She spoke in whispers, and Tommy did nothing to encourage a higher volume, not wanting to make his job superfluous. Feeling aggravated, Silver guessed at their conversation, like watching a mute TV from bed with dead batteries in the remote. The back of her shiny head, her tiny red nails on the counter, leather handbag hanging on forearm. Tommy's lips moved. "Name?" mouthed by that hole in the jelly-pouch. She hesitated. "Need a name for the book," he would be saying. Her head tilted low as she explained. Tommy nodded, speaking without looking at her; it wasn't good business to cause embarrassment. She turned toward the elevator, her cheek pink.

And now, Silver knew that she'd asked for a name already in the book, a registered guest. Tommy always asked for payment up front, and she hadn't paid, hadn't gotten a key to the room. Her lover was upstairs, waiting. This couldn't be her first time with him, maybe at the Belle Aire, maybe somewhere else, where he'd learned to trust her, arriving first and paying for the room, knowing she'd pay him back later.

Once she was safely in the elevator, Silver scowled at Tommy, who was pretending not to notice as he busily wrote in the book. *You bloodsucker—knew all along she was coming in and didn't tell me.* Tommy looked up, caught the glare and knew its meaning, but glanced at the elevator and back at Silver with a blasé expression, eyes wide enough to push up lumps of flesh. Silver approached the counter.

"You've seen these two before," he accused.

"First time," said Tommy.

Silver looked at him skeptically. "Who's the poke?"

Tommy grunted and shrugged his shoulders, sending a slow ripple from chest to belly. "The usual sort."

Silver regretted coming so close, the stench like old rendered fat. He debated whether to wait and see the gigolo for himself. Usually the man came down first, anxious to be on his way, while the lady stayed after to tidy herself. But sometimes it happened the other way. Silver had to be ready to move when she came down.

"The name?"

Tommy held out his hand, palm up. Silver removed his wallet from breast pocket, fingered the bills, and carefully extracted one of them. A pudgy fist gulped it. "Battle. Arlene Battle."

"Mr. and Mrs.?"

"Yeah. Who they foolin'? John and Arlene." Tommy smiled—the first time Silver had ever seen him smile—pushing a long-submerged dimple into his cheek. Silver had to smile too. Like living in the '30s instead of the

'70s, these women always gave Tommy a "name for the book" and almost always used their lover's surname. Modern sophistication had erased "Mr. and Mrs. John Smith," replacing them with a long list of other "married" couples in compliance with some unspoken, universal law of hotel occupancy.

Silver said nothing more, giving Tommy only his introspective, fleeting smile before returning to the lumpy chair. Now came the tense time, anticipation of the stalk. Soles planted in threadbare depressions, Silver leaned forward, forearms on knees, heels and toes alternately lifting and tapping. In the midst of his mental checklist, he pulled out his wallet and extracted the "G. Carroll Silver" card, then placed it loose in his breast pocket so he could extract it later in one easy and smooth movement.

That done, he continued down his list while his feet lifted and tapped. He forced a deep breath into his lungs and coughed it out. His rational side hoped to see the poke come down first, to learn a few details of appearance that could help him convince her. But his gut told him he didn't want to see the man who had freshly extracted himself from her body. Thoughts of what they'd been doing together only moments before often distracted Silver, causing him to slip when he first looked into her eyes and fought the real bear of his life. If business was to be had with this woman, the business he truly desired was the other man's.

Heels and toes, lifting and tapping. Five minutes passed. The elevator bell pinged and a couple came out laughing, walked through the lobby and into the revolving door. Another ten minutes. A man came in from the street, talked to Tommy, left. Seven or eight minutes more. A man Silver recognized as a dealer came in carrying a box-like attaché case, paid for a room, walked to the elevator. The bell spoke. "Arlene Battle" stepped out alone, and the dealer's head turned to her before he walked in. *Yeah, she's a looker all right; make you forget that kilo in your case.*

She headed for the door, her walk straight and direct yet easy, sated. She was the same in every way except for a lock of hair pushed out of place and a lack of concern for everyone she passed, the rest of the world. The moment she stepped into the revolving door, Silver jumped.

The street was crowded, and though he couldn't have been more than twenty feet behind, he lost sight of her the minute he stepped out of the revolving door. *Where the hell...?* He panicked and searched, cheeks slapped left and right. There she was, heading east with a deliberate, unhurried gait, now turning the corner. Silver rushed to catch up.

Part of the trick was in choosing the right moment, far enough from the hotel to startle her with the fact he'd been following for a distance, but close enough to avoid losing her to a moral separation from her recent escapade. It also helped to approach her near one of his spots for the talk, a place that would highlight the low level of her act. He had to make a split-second evaluation of personality. For some, a dirty coffee shop would do. For others, a bar worked better. But he couldn't misjudge. Some women became horrified, went running or worse—

clawed his neck.

Not this one. She and "John Battle" had been going at this for some time, Silver was sure of it. She would be immune to a lot of the dirt already, and so, for her, the lower the better.

Three blocks from the hotel, a red light stopped her at an intersection near one of Silver's favorite bars for the talk. The corner filled up with people heedless of the stop light, looking down the avenue in anticipation of a break in traffic that would allow them to make a run for it. The direction of her gaze joined theirs. Six, seven, eight people pushed in around her, now nine, now Silver. He squeezed through two bodies, coming directly behind and mere inches from her ear. The press of humanity, automobile fumes, rotting trash—none of it was strong enough to mask her rich fragrance, an exotic perfume.

"Mrs. Battle?"

She turned her head, not toward him, but away from the oncoming traffic to look straight ahead at the little red man. A moment in time, the two of them frozen while life teemed around them.

"Arlene?" he said, louder.

This time she turned to look at him, not noticing that the others disappeared, seconds before the red man became green.

He smiled the practiced, sly smile intended to communicate intimate knowledge. "Or should I use your real name?"

Now he saw the look, the eyes widening, the cheeks blanching, then flushing pink. Her eyes were more beautiful than he had imagined when watching her from afar.

Blue-gray, with natural dark, thick lashes.

"What do you want?" she asked, trying to sound indignant and superior, utterly failing. "Who are you?"

Silver neatly extracted his card with two fingers and handed it to her. She glanced at the card then looked at him with alarm in her eyes. "What are you investigating?"

"That's something maybe we should—"

"You've been following me, haven't you?" She looked at him hard when she asked the question. Her eyes filled with panic and skirted around his face to the sidewalk behind him, to the left, the right.

He followed suit, glancing everywhere, playing to her fear that she was standing out in the open, exposed. "Let's get off the street and talk about this, shall we?" He reached toward her elbow, touched it gently, then cupped it and turned her in the direction he wanted. *She's easy, she's mine.* Her thoughts were racing, he could sense it, but she hadn't yet put two and two together, otherwise she wouldn't let him lead her this way, she'd be asking more questions. The questions came once they got inside.

Her pupils still pinpoints from the midday sun, Arlene Battle couldn't immediately appreciate the full impact of their obscure den. Stunned and unaware, she allowed him to lead her to the bar, while her focus remained enclosed within a square foot of space. *Good, the place is nearly empty.* He motioned to a stool at the end of the bar. She sat, and he took the stool next to hers.

Something connected and Arlene suddenly looked at him accusingly. "If you're following me, why are you talking to me? Someone hired you. Who?"

"I think you already know."

She gulped. "My husband."

"Yes."

"Then why are you talking to me?" Her eyes shifted away from his as if her senses had awakened to the smell of stale smoke and whisky-soaked carpet, the sound of aging Bee Gees singing "Stayin' Alive" on a slow turntable. Her eyes had adjusted and now refocused on a spot about ten feet away where a sleepy dancer, clad only in sequined G-string, gyrated on top of the bar above a drooling, slack-jawed patron. Arlene's mouth opened and she averted her gaze but made no sign of running. Silver chuckled inside. *Pegged her right.*

But his expression bore only fatherly compassion for her and a baffled kind of wonder at himself. "Good question. I'm asking myself the same thing. You know, I've never done this before." He smiled humbly.

"Done what?"

"Well…" He was interrupted by the bartender, who instantly loomed before them, strongly suggesting they order drinks. *There goes another five at least, maybe six or seven.* He solicited his lady's desire. A mineral water for her, a Miller for him. The bartender promised a seltzer and Bud, then departed.

"I had to talk to you, now that I've seen you and followed you—"

"Has it been long?"

"Well, yes. Several days."

Her face fell and she dropped her head, shaking it. When she lifted it again, a tear was in her eye.

"Please don't get upset," he said. "Why do you think we're talking? Twenty-five years in this business and I can't figure it, but the God's honest truth is, I can't go back to your husband, knowing who he is and knowing you. I've seen a lot of things, and I can tell this isn't something you do casually."

She looked at him with new hope. "You don't know what he'd do! *Please* don't tell him. Promise me you won't!"

The bartender plunked down their glasses and gave them a curious look while he hovered, refusing to leave. Clearly, he required payment. Silver took out another of his precious twenties and prayed for the change as Arlene guided a quivering hand toward her drink, took a sip and nearly toppled the glass setting it down. The bartender loped off, not in a hurry to return.

Silver touched her elbow again, the velveteen coat she hadn't removed, and let his eyes roam downward. Nothing to see. *Unbutton it, Arlene, show me what you've got.* "Listen," he said. "Why do you think I stopped you? I told you, I don't want to give him my report. I can tell him you were too hard to tail, I lost you. He can think I'm a lousy detective, what do I care? Or I can make up some places you've been and maybe he'll believe me. It's just..."

"What is it?"

"With a report like that, he isn't gonna pay up. Even if he believes me, it isn't what he wants to hear. I have expenses, you know, per diem, three hundred bucks a day. He paid for two days but owes me for three more when I give the report. I mean, I don't like bringing this up, but I could've taken another job while I was running around after you."

"Don't worry about that. I'll pay you. Let me pay you. He owes you for three days? Nine hundred? Let me see what I have. I'll give you what he owes you, that way you won't even have to see him. If he calls, you can say you're off the case, you're on vacation, you've quit, whatever…" She fumbled with the clasp on her purse, then stopped and looked at him. "How do I know? How do I know you're telling the truth? What's going to stop you from telling him everything and taking his money too?"

Smart lady. Less than half of them ever got to that question, so upset were they at being followed, so relieved to find a way out. But what choice did she have, really? Payment was her only chance of salvation, even if it wasn't a guaranteed chance.

He had plenty of practice with this question and played the part well. He said nothing for several seconds while he looked at her with lifted brow and shrugged, then slid one foot down to the floor from its perch under the bar. "I'll put my hand on a Bible. What can I say? This is new to me too, I've never done anything like this. Look, maybe I can take a loss on one of the days, but three days—I don't know."

She searched his eyes, looking for the honesty he worked at communicating. The dancer, tucking a tip into her patch of cloth, bumped her way along the bar toward them, the click of her spike heels becoming audible. "Disco Inferno" came on like everything else, slowed a notch. Arlene looked up at the dancer and back at Silver then fumbled with the clasp on her purse again. "I'll pay you," she said. "I'll pay you, I have the nine hundred, just please don't deliver your report—" Her upper lip glistened and her eyelids fluttered. "Oh God! I have to— the ladies' room." She clapped a hand to her mouth, her eyes frantically searching the barroom. "Don't leave!" she screamed through her hand as she ran off toward the back.

Suddenly alone with the legs leading up to a crotch, Silver pondered his options. This was a new one, a mark getting sick on him in the middle of the deal. *I'll wait; didn't she tell me to wait? She's ready to pay.* He required cash and found it hard to believe she had the nine hundred in her purse. With some women he took what they had, with others he set up a meet for later in the day or the next day, as soon as they could get to the bank. He treated each one differently depending on his sense of the woman, her gullibility and intelligence.

At the beginning of this one he might have gone for a meet, but the way things were developing he wasn't sure. Too many questions, and now running off to the toilet. He didn't know if she would make it through all the intervening time, the hours to think, the act of withdrawing cash from her account as she reconsidered the sincerity of his assurances. Not a good risk. *I'll wait 'til she comes back and take what she's got, call it a day.*

Silver remembered his beer on the counter, untouched. He might as well drink it. He took a sip, noticing Arlene's glass of seltzer standing in a little pool of water with a lipstick imprint on the rim. He couldn't figure it, her running off sick like that. Maybe he'd mis- judged her from the start. She'd been a little flustered at the hotel with Tommy but nothing unusual, then so cool when she breezed out again, and almost confident with him in the beginning, demanding, "Who are you?" like he was a servant. Then, somehow, she'd started to crumble, tears in her eyes, a shaky voice, unable even to open her purse. Sweaty and pale, hand on her mouth.

"She's a Brick House" came on over the speakers, the woman above trying to convince him of just that. Silver looked up but not for long. Maybe Arlene wasn't so hard to figure. *This place is sickening.* He took a slug of the tepid beer and looked through the leggy inverted "V" at the bartender, who was finally coming his way with the change. The bartender slapped the bills on the counter between the dancer's heels and patted her on a bare cheek. Silver cringed, realizing she wouldn't leave until he gave her something. Of course he could walk away, but he'd decided to wait. *Maybe I should go in the back, hang out by the head. How long does it take to vomit anyway?* Under the counter, he took a single dollar bill out of his change and folded it, hoping the dancer wouldn't notice when he handed it up. She bent low to receive it. Winked. Bumped on her way.

Silver folded and shoved the rest of his change into a pants pocket and took another gulp, feeling the churning combination of coffee, bread, and beer in his stomach. Had it been five minutes or twenty-five? He hadn't checked his watch, and something about the darkness in the middle of the day and the plodding, slowed beat of the music made time stand still and seem like an eternity all at once. One disco number after another had played but he hadn't been counting. He took another gulp and the beer was gone. Now he was sure something was up.

He pushed away from the bar and made his way to the back where he found a narrow, short hallway with a pay phone at one end, the men's and ladies' rooms on either side. The odor was overpowering and the carpet seemed wet under his shoes—but Arlene would have waited until she was over the can. He stood next to the ladies' door and listened. No gagging or coughing sounds, no toilet flushing, no water running, but a shuffling noise and a click of heels on a tile floor.

"Arlene?" he called, not too loudly. "You all right in there?"

The heels clicked toward the door, the bolt lock turned, the door opened slowly. The bright light of the bathroom formed a halo behind her head, leaving her face obscure. She seemed different, taller, very calm. Silver's heart dropped like a stone in his chest.

"I'm sorry," she said, stepping forward slowly in a frozen frame—a single step he would always remember. Her movement toward him released the bathroom light into his eyes. *She can see me.* Silver felt the changes in his face: the sudden paleness followed by a slow flush.

Then the metal was tight around his left wrist squeezing it bloodless, the other cuff secured through a hole in the steel box casing of the pay phone. She slapped another pair of cuffs on his right wrist and one of his belt loops while he stood docile, wondering why he was allowing this to happen. Only when he was fastened in place, speechless and helpless, did he notice her coat, un-buttoned to reveal, at last, what was underneath: a police shield on a chain around her neck; a shoulder holster unsnapped, the butt of a gun available under her left breast; a tape recorder strapped to her waist.

She talked while she frisked him. "It won't be long now Mr. Silver—or should I call you by your real name?" She smiled and looked him in the eye. "I've called my backup. They're just around the corner. You're under arrest, in case you're wondering."

She continued the frisk. "The big P.I. doesn't have a gun, eh?" She was holding his possessions—his wallet, his keys, the loose bills from his pocket. She opened the wallet and looked inside, frowned, and put everything in her handbag, not having difficulty opening it this time. "You have the right to remain silent; anything you say can be used against you."

Her warning aside, he had much to say but couldn't speak. He replayed the events of the past hour, searching for the clue he had missed, coming up empty yet finding the incongruous conclusion that none of it was surprising, everything leading to this one, logical ending point. He had always supposed that some people might find what he did objectionable or wrong, even illegal. In fact, he knew it was illegal. *But it's so right for these women. Can't she see how right it is for me to step in and deliver them from danger, every one of them so wanting and willing and beautiful and grateful? Doesn't any of that count? Doesn't it count that I do it for them?*

"You don't understand," he told her softly.

"Oh yes, I do. You're the scum of the earth, Silver." She was tough and abrasive then, not an ounce of the woman she'd been at the start. And he despised her.

She swiveled to look out of their little hallway toward the bar area. Silver looked too. Miraculously, life went on with the handful of people in there, none of them seeming to notice what was going on in the back.

"Oh, hell! Where *is* my backup? Guess they're just not coming!" Arlene flashed a playful look at Silver, a glint in her eye, causing the blood to drain from his face a second time. As the blood rushed back, she sent a laugh through the air that confirmed his suspicions and revealed what he'd missed.

He recognized her, recognized himself. Too late. She turned and was gone.

Silver waited.

And waited.

≋CHASING HAWKS

THEY WERE SOMEWHERE in Wyoming, about to make another pit stop, when Sammy glanced south and said, "Better get that thing checked." They hadn't been together a month, and she'd been holding it in about his frequency problem. And other things.

Still, they both knew she wouldn't be running away after what went down in Colorado. They had a new, easy way with each other. So he took what she said in the way she intended, as a joke with just a little bit of the truth.

"Be my guest," he answered, with a twist of a grin.

When they first met, Sammy guessed he was fifty or so but didn't ask. She was coming into that time of life when she started to notice things that people never talked about, or if they did, she'd never had reason to listen. He was the first man to open a window on a future she'd just as soon ignore with all the unpleasant unknowns to come. Years ago, every discovery was transformative, crazy, astonishing, food for the curious, but Sammy was forty-seven now and already beginning to tire of living, the unexpected things just turning out bad.

Anyway. From the get-go, she decided to give him a chance. There'd been a slew of others, her longest three being Skeez, Hinto, and Carlos, a Goth, Dakota, and Mexican. First lay, common law, and husband (ex). She'd dumped Carlos six months ago after an endless green card odyssey—her gift to a man she couldn't understand. With Carlos, like all of them, it was the mystery that first drew her in but later repelled her when the gloss wore thin over the common grunt underneath.

A man had to have an edge or he was nothing. A few had come close, but she was still waiting. The best of them had teased her up to the precipice, daring to survive a plunge to the gully—but they always pulled back in sorry retreat for the main road.

Her new man was Walt, a mutt of sorts like herself, dark skin and a nameless, messy ancestry. A ridiculous name, "Walter," to go along with it. In the same way, Sammy's umber-colored Mama had tried to change her baby's chances with a fancy name. "Samantha" jumped off a glossy magazine cover in the clinic waiting room, where she sat with the eight-month fetus stuck high up in her belly. Mama's baby, as soon as she was old enough to attract a man, always introduced herself with the full version of her name, pronouncing it like a girl it should properly belong to. "Hello, I'm Samantha." She would stretch it out, all a test.

This man, Walt, had passed the test immediately. "No, you're not." His New Mexican desert eyes threw heat, impressing her with the quickness of his knowing her.

"I'm not?" she pretended.

"I'm calling you Sammy." Just like that, no question.

He was her first astonishing discovery in a dozen years. Their barbed undersides were identical, she sensed it and stuck with that ticket for the first few weeks while keeping alert for signs that their invisible glue might turn into a sappy sameness.

His frequency problem and the threat of ordinariness weren't entirely obvious until the road trip. He was taking her back to South Dakota, her home state, away from her stopping place of the last eight years, New Mexico. He was a traveling man, he said, and never stayed in one place for very long, but he'd never seen South Dakota, and didn't she want to go back? "Sure, as long as you're not asking to see the presidents' heads." He looked at her like she was crazy, and so she knew it was safe.

He wasn't aware—she hadn't told him—about the years just ended with the Mexican and all the favors he'd squeezed from her with a grab and yank of her forearm, a thunder roll in the bed. Many midnights she put up with his houseguests, cousins and friends, dusty bodies reeking of darkness, sweat, and hunger, the excitement and danger of it all just a temporary cover for the commonness of peonage, dollars, tortillas, and dead ends. Abandoned families. She didn't want to stay and remember.

Sammy first met Walt at the Coyote Grill when she shoved a beer his way along the bar, sending a smooth layer of froth over the edge and down the side. They started up that night, after closing. Less than a month later he made the offer, right in the middle of her shift at the Coyote. No need to think it through. She wasn't sentimental. Sammy announced to all within hearing range that she was quitting and walked right out of the joint into the parking lot, where Walt sat idling his Barracuda convertible. She jumped in, never to look back.

He had money, it was sure, but she didn't know the source and liked her ignorance of it better. She reserved a place in her mind for the shimmer of gold suspended over the canyon, his grab for it as they walked the edge, pushing a dry tumble of dirt and rocks down. Down.

Mid May, good and hot with the top down.

Five minutes out, he confessed. "This is good for me."

"Good how?"

"Have to get out of N.M."

"Me exactly."

"No, you don't get it."

"I get it. Believe me, I get it."

"I got people after me."

"We all do. I get it."

And he started talking, on and on, about a sweet deal that went sour for someone else, while Sammy turned her face northeast into the hot wind, letting it buffet her cheeks and tangle her curls and drown out most of his story with all its drama, the same kind of story that sooner or later would just come up short of ordinary. His was a good one, though, a sophisticated mind-fuck of a swindle, but all the same...

She threw a word in here or there to build it. "With a car like this, they're bound to find you."

"No one touches this car."

"Sure thing."

"I'll kill the sonuva..."

"You bet." And she threw him a smile. She banked on the prettiness of her mouth, and he liked her smiles, especially that first one over the spilt beer at the Coyote.

Pale blue. A vast empty expanse of it lay between them and the searing white disk hovering overhead. Nothing else. It could have been painted there, ripped from a paper ceiling, proving they didn't exist. None of it did. Best to lean back in the seat and feel the wind and hope to catch sight of something, an eagle, a cloud, a slight incline, a tumble weed, a curve in the highway.

Sammy gripped the top of the passenger door and laid her forearm along the length of the window well, the metal shank dangerously hot from baking in the sun. The bright yellow 'cuda was a fine automobile alright, and a mystery man had asked her to take a long ride in it.

Up from the border it was Las Cruces, then a stop in Truth or Consequences. They'd been only two hours on the road. "You need it?" he asked. "No," and she waited in the car outside the QuickStop or some such, not thinking anything of it. Not yet. But it took him a little longer than she would have liked.

Coming up on Los Lunas the sign said, "Correctional Facility Ahead/Do Not Pick Up Hitchhikers," and after that, the barbed wire and guard tower could be seen well off the road, but then, Walt couldn't hang on much past Santa Fe and made another stop.

"Want something?"

"A Coke," she said, helping him out with an excuse, helping herself out with her plan, not yet scuttled, to give this one a chance. Maybe the Coke would be enough to make her go in the next putrid hole, standing, just like

Walt, a slave to the drip.

The minute he stepped away from the car she could see the end coming. The dry excitement of his big swindle wouldn't hold her, and his attraction to gas-station toilets revealed his stinginess with money. He could afford to stop somewhere nice with an air-conditioned booth. She was restless, jittery, her insides pressing out against the tick tock, wanting to be on the move where everything was fine because the gazing out was a kind of puzzle that somehow took the place of the need for danger. Or maybe it suggested the danger she needed.

He came back with more than just Cokes, a bag of shrink-wrapped sponge and cardboard she knew she would eat anyway. Next up was Raton, N.M., then over the border into Colorado, "No Jake Brakes Beyond this Point," almost to Trinidad and another stop, this time for gas on top of the usual thing. Still, she wouldn't get out of the car. But this time, when he came back and started up again, he did something unexpected. He turned off the interstate.

She said something to build it. "You're going wrong, baby. This is due west." The 'cuda took the curves all right with a bright ball in her eyes, two hours from sunset.

"Better to shake it up," he said. She knew. "Just a little detour." She could guess. "I know someone in Ludlow and don't want to meet up with him."

"Same one?"

"Different."

She would play along and imagine all the swindled marks and their gleaming blades lurking at every outpost.

They climbed, getting closer to the mountains, and it

was god-awful beautiful. "Not For Sale, Don't Even Ask." Then "Entering God's Country." It had been seven or eight hours, and finally she was the one to ask for a stop because it was crisp and clean and Mary mother of Jesus God's country. He pulled off the road into the red dust and pebbles. She saw green pine needles and white clouds in a bright blue and a little grove, secluded, walking distance, no one to see. She went off this time on her own into the little stand of trees, took a tissue out of her pocket, toed off her sandals, ripped her jeans and thong clear off the end of her legs, and propped a foot hip-high against a tall pine.

She used the tissue and, still naked from the waist down, walked over to another tree, enjoying the breeze on her bare legs and other places. Leaning her back against the tree, she looked up into the little circle of sky framed by the treetops.

This was just it. He couldn't see her inside the trees, but he could use a little imagination. Ten years ago, even five, no man she'd ever been with would've left her naked backside alone under these circumstances. Still he didn't come. To hell with him.

A red-tailed hawk soared over and disappeared behind the tree cover so fast, it could have been a dream. Seconds later it turned back and came into view, not in a lazy soar but madly flapping with two tiny birds in pursuit. Swallows maybe? Each a tenth of the size of the raptor. They disappeared and reappeared again and again, a performance of foolish bravado meant for her. The weak were the strong, risking death, darting in to threaten and peck at the skirt of the hawk's wings, no fear of the talons and the hooked beak and the blood thirst of the predator.

"Hey!" she heard from a distance. She ignored him and kept her eyes up, hoping to see the birds again. They'd disappeared.

"Need help in there?" he called out.

She could hear in his voice that he thought he was being clever and he wouldn't be coming in. She pulled her clothes on and sauntered out of the woods, finding him propped against the passenger side, staring her down as she approached. He didn't move, so she went right up to him, not breaking their eye lock but not letting him know she was interested, a little punishment for his failure to pursue. He made it up a little by grabbing the back of her neck and pulling her in and showing her it was good for something else too. He tasted of metal and smelled of the sun.

"What were you doing in there?"

"Watching a hawk."

"I saw it too."

"Well?" She was laid up against his body, propped on the door. A car took the curve on the road behind them.

"Might've threatened the nest," he said.

"Defending their territory?"

"Something like that. Hey." She was moving and could tell he liked it. Another car went by. He kissed her again and pushed them up to standing. "Wait'll I get you." He spanked her rear and walked around front to the driver's side. "We'll get some food and a room in the Springs."

Teasing can be a kicker, sure, and the final reward even better, but this time it didn't make up for the notch he'd just dropped closer to ordinary. He gunned the engine and stirred up the red dust behind them to find the asphalt.

She pushed back in the seat and held her head on the start button of a migraine. The road was just as gorgeous but steadily more winding and nauseating and the mass in her gut was wearing off, pulling a hunger grumble into the mix. A detour, he said, and they'd be back on the interstate before she knew it, but in less than an hour he was pulling onto another dusty shoulder near another stand of trees, his own private john. "Right back," he said.

She sat, piano playing the chrome with stabbing, quick fingertips. Angry now, and hungry, and kicking herself for foolishness in the dusty gray at the merge of day and night. The sun was nearly down and hidden by the trees, any color of sunset withheld from her and given to the rest of the world out on the flat expanse left behind. Why that man hadn't done this back in her little grove…

The road was quiet, the engine ticked. Her digits, hard as hail balls, pecked and recoiled, bouncing on the metal.

It was then she heard the engine coming up behind. In the rearview she saw it, a black 4 by 4 with enormous wheels and the growl of a tank, nosing around the curve, slowing, pulling onto the dirt, creeping up and stopping close on the 'cuda's tail. It was an aggressive vehicle, driven by a man with an edge. Had to be.

Sammy's eyes skated from the empty ignition to the motionless stand of trees. Good, she thought. Why? Here was her chance to see what she could do on her own. A chance to see how it would change when Walt emerged from the woods, zipping his fly.

A big man, a match for the truck, climbed down from the driver's seat, passed behind the Barracuda over to the passenger side and came up on her like a trip back in time. Her pulse quickened the way it should, making her ready for him.

Her right hand gripped the top of the door. She wouldn't move it, but neither did he take heed of the warning, placing his two hands to the right and left of hers. He leaned in with his tree stump of a neck under a square, unshaven jaw. First it was the bare, bulldog arms she saw, then the mouth, a harelip and exposed teeth.

"You," he said.

"What of it?"

"Where's your man?"

She smirked and moved her eyes up from his mouth, letting him imagine what was in them.

"Nice car he's got." Slapped it, right next to her hand.

Still she said nothing and didn't look away.

"Nice woman he's got."

"Careful now."

"Back in Trinidad—"

She lifted her eyebrows.

"I saw you. I know you."

"You're not that lucky."

"What's your name?"

"Samantha."

"No, it's not."

"Right about that," said Walt behind him.

The man twisted his head back, then turned full around and took a step away from Sammy, toward the hood. "You," he said.

"Right about that too." Walt, a head shorter, pushed up into the man's chest, catching him off guard and making him stumble back, laughing.

This man—Walt's recent mark? Maybe not. Maybe he was the one from Ludlow, or another from a long-forgotten swindle. Or maybe he was no one at all, just a man from Trinidad who'd seen what he liked, sitting pretty and alone in a bright yellow Barracuda with the top down. She enjoyed that thought. But if he was the mark from N.M., the only impressive thing about his muscle was what it said about Walt, a man cunning enough to fell the bull.

For an eye blink everything held in the balance, a seesaw poised on the tip of now. One move and the past would go up and the future would come crashing down to where she could take off running.

She caught Walt's eye. He saw it too. They could own this and earn their night in the Springs and have the next day together, Sammy ribbing him at the pit stop in Lusk WY. Everything would be turned to fun with the proving behind them, until the next time.

A vein throbbed in Walt's temple, a dozen heartbeats the measure of what was to happen next.

Sammy climbed on the seat and hopped over like a colt. It was the two of them now, Walt and Sammy. What did they have? Yet a flash of fallen light.

When she sprang, the man recoiled, adjusted his vision, changed his mind. "Whoa!" He bucked up his taut shoulders. Sammy wanted to touch that power, just once, before it happened.

She stepped in, smiled, and deflected. Walt grabbed at something in his thigh and brought it up in a clenched fist, a silent weapon of blood, sinew, and bone.

The man stepped forward to meet it. In a cloud of red dust, they took him down.

ᨠTHE PIANO TEACHER'S LOVER

AT A TIME when everything he did was flung into moral doubt, Palmer Kittredge found comfort in a single, reassuring thought—a vision of her, his earliest impression.

That first day, Palmer had arrived home earlier than usual to find the girl in his living room. She sat near the edge of the sofa cushion, legs bent at a perfect right angle with music books on her school-uniform-skirted lap, head turned toward the closed door of the studio. He'd made enough noise to be noticed, dropping his car keys on the hall table and letting his briefcase slip to the floor, but she didn't seem to hear.

Forgetting his usual habit—the casual stride, the insincere "hello"—Palmer froze within a still pocket of air, slowly awakening to a magnificent sound emanating from the studio. The music was simple and tragic, a Brahms intermezzo played flawlessly and with a maturity rarely heard in the house except from Elizabeth. But this was not Elizabeth. Palmer intimately knew her interpretations, equal to this one in magnificence but gentler and more reserved in tone. This player gave the piece a

49

heavier reading, finding ominous shadings beneath the romantic melody.

Palmer listened, motionless, unable to take his eyes off the girl, who remained perched like an aerialist balanced on a trapeze. Her posture communicated intelligence and inviolability, but the intensity of her focus on the studio door permitted his gaze. In this way she was receptive, he imagined, or felt without imagining, as he continued to stare, vaguely apprehensive and guilty but feeling accepted and forgiven all the same.

The piece came to a close. For a while longer, the two listeners remained as they were while another sound filled the void. Elizabeth's voice, muffled but clearly appreciative, drifted out to them from behind the closed door. At last, the girl turned to Palmer. Their eyes met and her look was direct and unafraid, without embarrassment. It was a look to remember.

"Wasn't that beautiful?" she declared.

"Yes. Certainly. Very beautiful."

And he was struck by the presence of her, a young girl on the brink of adulthood, inexperienced in life's hard lessons yet capable of appreciating a fine thing. Such a fine thing!

That was a Wednesday, a spring evening, the first time Palmer had ever paid more than the usual passing notice to anyone in his living room. He'd come to expect strangers in the house, Elizabeth's piano students and their family members, blending in with the decor like additional sticks of furniture. They were trained to enter without knocking or ringing the bell (the noise would disrupt any lesson in progress), and would settle in the living room, which doubled as a waiting area for the adjacent studio. A closed door between the two rooms partially muffled the imperfect Bach and Beethoven.

As a defense against this encroachment on his privacy, Palmer had acquired an indifference toward the clientele, together with the compensating habit of uttering a pleasant greeting as he stepped from the foyer and strode through the living room, making his way into outlying regions of the house. Complete avoidance was difficult. He supposed that, after parking his car in the detached garage, he could enter the house through the kitchen, but pride wouldn't allow him to sneak in the back door like a thief or a mere hireling.

Many faces became familiar, but Palmer had never made an attempt to coordinate his schedule with any of theirs. As a rule, Elizabeth's students—mostly children—were required to attend once a week at the same time, but schedules were often made to be broken.

This constant grappling with uncertainty was Elizabeth's chief complaint about her line of work. "Patty needs to reschedule because of a conflict with Girl Scouts of all things, but the only open slot is Tuesday at three, that is, if Tommy plans to skip this week, as his mother said he might." Or some such nonsense all the time. Busy children, busy families, discounting the importance of musical training, relegating it to number three or four on the list of necessary extracurricular activities. Elizabeth, who'd never been a mother, didn't fully understand, often taking their meager enthusiasm as a personal affront.

Although Palmer was sensitive to her feelings (his

passion for music nearly as intense), he understood the other side of the argument as well, having been through all of it with growing children in his former life. Back then, scheduling had always been Irene's job, although it was Palmer, according to his ex-wife, who'd set the standards and priorities by which the schedules were made. Irene would arrange everyone's lives down to the minute only to have Palmer throw a wrench into her carefully laid plans with one of his offhand comments: "You know, Irene, Danny really should be getting more exercise." Casual observation or inflexible requirement? Irene always understood the latter.

In truth, Palmer's outlook varied little from Irene's— a mere difference in style, not substance—but petty arguments and small injuries had a way of adding up over the years. Throughout it all, Palmer secretly disparaged Irene's obsession over the minutia of daily existence, a sign of her underlying angst about mortality, while he maintained a free conscience, sure that he suffered from no such anxiety. There she was, ticking off the hours, checking the checklist, using her own formula to measure success in life with exact quantities of science, art, music and physical activity. According to Palmer, children needed to explore without the straitjacket of a schedule. They were sponges, eager, bright, and receptive, to be plopped down in a pool of basic values and healthy activity, soaking it all in, growing ever more succulent and wise.

Whenever he thought like this, Palmer grew nostalgic for his children, Daniel and Caitlin, now in college setting their own priorities. The one regret in his life was having missed so many of their teen experiences, left to decipher them piecemeal during awkward weekend and summer visits under the court-ordered schedule (yet another schedule engineered by Irene and her lawyer). In theory, now that the children were of age, the schedule was lifted, and Palmer was free to see them when he wished. But they rarely called, and their need for him seemed questionable enough that he frequently went for months without summoning the energy to take the first step.

All those living room guests, so different in age, shape and size, nevertheless took on similar characteristics, the indicia of impatience or distraction. Mothers, fathers, and nannies pretended to be reading a novel or the newspaper, and fidgeting children found it difficult to sit still while awaiting their lessons. Each one would look up as Palmer entered, some smiling or saying "hello," others looking away immediately as if he weren't there, a twinge of guilt and embarrassment in their eyes. They'd no reason to feel guilty. They were complying with protocol, Elizabeth's expectation that they remain.

But, after all, they were sitting in someone else's living room, and that someone else, the piano teacher, now obviously had a personal life to go along with the professional. A man coming home. A husband. Although Palmer wasn't a husband. He'd resisted another marriage.

The girl was the first one, the only one, who didn't look up. She sat listening, and when the music ceased, she made the comment about its beauty, and then just sat, eyes widening on Palmer's response. Her dark hair was long, held back neatly with a headband, combed smooth and falling in perfect layers like sculpted marble over the curves of her shoulders and back. Her proud, young torso was long and erect. Into Palmer's mind came a picture of his own daughter at the same age: a fall morning, chill in the house, Caitlin, hair freshly combed, wearing a translucent nightgown, opening the bathroom door in a rush of sunlight from the window behind her, forming a nimbus around the gauzy outline of flesh.

The girl spoke into this image. "Who are you?"

He was taken aback by the question, so sudden, so unselfconscious. Unnecessary too, it would seem. Who was he? Wasn't it obvious? The piano teacher's lover.

But it wasn't obvious to the girl, who was asking a logical question with every right to learn the answer. *I'm the piano teacher's husband*, he could have said with a proper sound to avoid causing alarm. But, "I live here," is what he did say, not wishing to lie.

"I thought so," she said.

"My name is Palmer. What's yours?" He found it easy to converse with the girl.

"Maruta," she said.

"Maruta?"

"Yes. You said it right."

"How wonderful. Maruta."

He hesitated before taking two steps toward the sofa, as if intending to sit next to her, when the studio door opened. Out stepped a boy of about sixteen and Elizabeth, close behind. Her heart had pumped the blood up into her cheeks in a way that seemed familiar but forgotten. At first she didn't see Palmer, the end point of her vision pressed into the back of the boy's neck. The boy had Maruta's erect bearing and dark hair, although his was curly. This was, had to be, Maruta's older brother.

Elizabeth's eyes floated past the boy's shoulders and caught in a fast hold on Palmer. "Home early?" she asked, not much interested, although the mere fact of a question marked the occasion. Ordinarily, if she'd caught him in the living room on his way to another part of the house, she would have said nothing. But this time, perhaps his intention to remain was obvious.

"Um-hmm," he responded.

"We've just finished up."

"No lesson for you?" Palmer addressed Maruta.

"I've already had mine."

"Come on," said the older brother. "Let's see if Mom is waiting." At that moment, he seemed entirely too young to have produced the wonderful music they'd heard only moments before.

Palmer stepped to the front window and saw a station wagon pulling up front at the curb. Following Palmer's example, the boy looked out the window and said, "She's here," then, "thank you," to Elizabeth in a way that matured him suddenly.

"See you next week, Vadin," said Elizabeth.

Proudly, as if balancing a dictionary on her head, Maruta rose from the cushion, said goodbye to Elizabeth, and gave Palmer a look identical to the first one she'd given him. Her deliberate attentiveness seemed so clear to him, but happened so quickly, it likely meant nothing at all. Palmer confirmed this with a quick appraisal of Elizabeth's face. Not a hint of awareness.

When the door closed behind brother and sister,

Palmer made the effort to remove his eyes from the window. He threw a forced smile Elizabeth's way as he passed her and walked into the bathroom, where he stood dumbly, looking at himself in the mirror until another student arrived and started up in the studio. During that lesson and the two that followed, he went on about his business in the house and ate alone, saving a plate for Elizabeth on the counter.

Hours later, in bed, in the dark, he said to her, "You never told me about them," surprised to hear an undercurrent of accusation in his voice.

She didn't ask him to explain. She knew immediately. "Well, you don't usually come home that early."

"True. But that boy…"

"Vadin."

"…he's exceptional. Seems you would have mentioned him."

"He's only been coming a few months." As if that explained it all.

There was a silence before Elizabeth spoke. "It's a pity, though. She's no good at all. Has none of her brother's talent."

Palmer smiled to think that Elizabeth needed to add this. He touched her hand, but it remained limp. He curled his fingers over the top and into the palm, then lifted it, pulling her arm up over her head, leaving an entire side of her open and defenseless. He leaned over her body and took the other hand, pulling it up overhead in a similar manner, pinning it down on the pillow. They fell easily and quickly into each other. Their lovemaking was simple, quiet, and unimaginative but fully satisfying to them both within the cushion of their individual, private thoughts.

Just as easily, they fell away from each other, their quickened breath the only audible sound. Elizabeth's heart had pumped the blood up into her face, but the room was dark and Palmer didn't see.

Alice and Vaughn were over for dinner the following Saturday, and everyone was sipping their third glass of wine (a rare vintage Palmer had discovered on his last trip to Provence), when he advised his guests: "I wouldn't dismiss anything she says or writes as nonsense. Children are wiser than we know—we have to regard them as adults in youthful disguise."

"And adults are mere babes in wrinkled skin," observed Vaughn.

"Well, try to remember how it felt to be fifteen, when everything was important and life was so dramatic and we were so smart."

"Or thought we were."

"Palmer means smart mouthed, I'm sure that's what he means, don't you, Palmer?" Alice, flippant.

Palmer ignored her—he often ignored Alice—and said, "No, really, think about it, here we all are, pushing fifty…"

"Speak for yourself." Vaughn, indignant at forty-six.

"…decades of memory stuffed into overloaded brains, suffering from those little embarrassing episodes of senility—"

"Speak for yourself."

"—while *they* have vast expanses of untapped

territory, absorbing, just sucking it in with curiosity and interest. Such emotional, intelligent sponges."

"There go those *sponges* again," droned Elizabeth.

"Palmer, the water's dripping out your ears," laughed Alice, raising her glass.

"At fifty, absorbed too damn much." Vaughn.

"Only forty-nine," corrected Palmer.

"And senile already! Tsk, tsk. What's this all about, Palm? Feeling your mortality?"

"I just wish they'd give some of it back," said Elizabeth. "If they're absorbing so much while they're practicing—*if* they *are* practicing—I never hear it. No thought, no sensitivity."

"That's just it. They're not wise and reflective," said Alice. "Just emotional. All that misdirected emotion."

"Rushing through every piece. Must be those teenage hormones." Elizabeth looked at Palmer and he returned: "But not that Vadin. Sensitive and slow." Bouncing his eyebrows up and down like Groucho.

"Vah-deen," she corrected him.

"*Vaaaahhhh-deeeen!*"

"They're smart without being wise. That's the difference," said Alice, holding her glass out to Palmer. "And so open to suggestion. That's what worries me about Michelle. She absorbs everything just like you say, but she keeps it all in and obsesses over God knows what."

"You know, this is the thing," said Palmer, pouring. "Every other parent of a teenager is worried they'll come home and find drugs and sex going on in the house, and you, you two," he waved his glass, "worry about how much Shakespeare Michelle is reading while you're gone! I don't get it—"

"It's not just that, Palm."

"I don't get it! Your theory about smart, not wise. All the reading and writing she does, that girl is wiser than any of us!"

"Palmer!" They were all shouting at once. Vaughn won the match. "Her room is floor to ceiling boxes of sheets and notebooks of her writing, most of which she doesn't let us see…"

"But the *ones* we've *seen!*" screeched Alice.

"Strings of unconnected words, no meaning to any of it! One sick image after another, almost obscene sounding without any obscenity—"

"Purely schizophrenic, and she can't explain any of it when we ask!"

"Maybe she doesn't want to," interjected Palmer. "I wouldn't worry. Poetry isn't about the literal meaning anyway, but the sounds, the images, the suggestions…"

"Palmer is such an authority on poetry." From Elizabeth, tongue-in-cheek.

Vaughn sat up and brought the glass stem down hard on the table. "Why didn't I think of it! Palmer's a writer! He should read Michelle's poetry!"

"Such an authority."

"I only do nonfiction and travel," said Palmer. "Haven't written a stitch of poetry."

"I'm just saying, you know, a little meeting, writer to writer, the mature older one as the mentor, giving some guidance to a confused kid. Get her to open up a little and explain it. You know damn well kids don't talk to their own parents."

"Damn well," said Palmer. He drained his glass, and for the first moment in a long evening there was silence at the table, an awareness of red eyes, incipient headaches, rumpled clothing, the creeping of age. Suddenly, with the reverberation of a closing vault door, there was a need for rest, the thought of bed.

"Bring her to me, then," said Palmer, quietly.

The whole point of Palmer's current lifestyle, so he thought, had been to remain as unscheduled yet responsible as necessary. Five years ago he'd quit everything—Irene, family life, a staff post he'd held for twelve years—and ventured out on his own as a freelancer, establishing a single, private office, his sanctuary. Shortly after that, he'd taken up with Elizabeth.

An underlying insecurity, which he didn't care to admit, had caused him to work long hours and to travel entirely too much, keeping him away from home, when most of his work could be done locally with a little online research, supplemented by file photos and his memory of past trips. Now that his travel column was syndicated, he was assured of a certain, adequate income and could afford to take it easier.

Still, he hadn't let up, and he regarded his fortuitous meeting with the girl, Maruta, as a sign of an inner hypocrisy he now found unattractive in himself. No, he hadn't arranged his schedule in any deliberate manner, but now he began to see how, perhaps, he had. He'd become a slave to primitive fears over the source of his next meal as a means of avoiding the busiest time in his home, the strangers he didn't particularly care to meet.

Funny how he'd always been attracted to people in faraway lands—places he didn't belong—while feeling slightly repelled by the strangers in his own home (really Elizabeth's four walls in title). What he'd always justified as mere indifference toward these people was really a mild form of repulsion, similar in fact to the feeling he'd experienced in the last years coming home to Irene and the kids—people who weren't strangers at all! Yet Maruta was different, a foreigner who didn't negate his sense of belonging.

With these thoughts circulating, not yet congealed, and without any specific, conscious recollection of the date and time, Palmer arrived home the second Wednesday even earlier than the first. Still not early enough to hear Maruta play—she was sitting as before, waiting for Vadin—but at the moment he saw her, Palmer thought, *yes, of course, Maruta is here*, recognizing the perfection of his timing. She and her brother, naturally, were among that rare class of clients who could be counted on to keep their appointments, and Palmer had arrived in their schedule precisely near the start of Vadin's lesson, Maruta's concluded, with enough time to begin a conversation.

She didn't look up when he entered, but this time there was something new—the slightest movement of her arm, a shifting of weight on the cushion, a strand of hair falling from her shoulder—what, he didn't know exactly, making it evident to him that she noticed his entrance. This time he didn't pause, but walked up to the couch and hovered nearby, not wanting to sit unless he received a sign of invitation.

Almost immediately, the sign came. She turned to him and smiled, her lovely face blurred in a frame of rippling Debussy arpeggios. "Hello," she said.

"Hello." He took his cue and sat down, leaving three feet of space between them. "Your brother is quite a remarkable player."

"Yes, he is." Her smile became spiritual, a look of reverence, acceptance, truth. Not a shred of sibling jealousy. In his own, former household, any reference to Daniel's talents used to send Caitlin, the younger, into a pouting snit of indignation, punctuated with allegations of favoritism.

"Maruta," he said, as if testing his memory, though he knew he was right. "And your brother is Vadin?"

She nodded.

"What is the origin of your names?" Despite his years of travel and familiarity with several tongues, Palmer was genuinely at sea.

She didn't answer immediately but looked straight into his eyes, as if considering the potential consequences of her answer. "My mother made them up."

"Made them up?"

"Yes. The first two letters of my name are for the month of my birth, when flowers are blooming. She says I reminded her of a budding hyacinth when she first saw me. The 'root' sound is for stability and tenacity. And she added the 'a' at the end to make it sound prettier."

The explanation was her mother's, he knew, but she'd made the words her own. "Interesting," he said. "A unique name, just for you! And Vadin? What does that mean?"

She paused and looked at the studio door. *L'Isle Joyeuse* was coming to a close. "You'll have to ask him."

Palmer respected her sudden silence and waited until the piece had finally concluded and the soft mumble of conversation had begun behind the studio door.

"I assumed your names were from a particular country or nationality."

"Nationality? I don't know of any."

"One of the Baltic nations, or maybe Pakistan?"

"We're from the United States."

"Yes, of course."

"We're North American, you could say."

Palmer was silenced, could do nothing but smile meekly like a defeated game show contestant. He searched her eyes and found forgiveness.

"What country would you have said I was from?" she asked.

"Oh, I don't know. Your answer is the only thing that makes sense. You're from here. You belong here."

She nodded thoughtfully and looked at him, almost surprised. "Your name isn't so easy either."

"Yes, well, Palmer. It's easy enough to say."

"What kind of name is that?"

"English."

"So, you're from England?" She smiled in a way that said she was pulling his leg.

He laughed in amazement. Wise beyond her years! "No, not the least bit English," he said with a British accent.

"So, you're North American? You belong here."

He paused in a rut of indecision. "I don't know," he said. "I'd say that's debatable."

Elizabeth couldn't have known they'd been talking. Shortly before Vadin's lesson was up, Palmer's internal clock told him to get up and walk into the kitchen. He hadn't planned it that way, nor could he say why he didn't wish Elizabeth to know, but he was sensitive to the signs that the end was near—the extended, muffled talk from behind the closed door, discussion about assignments for next week—and he stood, excusing himself politely, and walked away.

He'd learned much in their twenty-five minutes together. The girl's mother was devoted to her children to the point of suffocation, but Maruta spoke of her with such love and admiration she seemed to thrive under her mother's watchful eye. The woman was obviously intelligent and artistic—the names of her children alone proved it. Vadin was a scholar and a prodigious composer. "That's Vadin's music," Maruta said proudly when an unfamiliar melody drifted out to them from the studio. She revered her brother just short of idolization, and Vadin protected her, while respecting her maturity and intelligence.

Without really knowing these people, Palmer felt the symbiotic pull of need and love, which hadn't stifled and confined Maruta but had set her free, strengthening her to an astonishing level of maturity. There was no talk of a father. It seemed she had none, but Palmer didn't want to know and didn't ask, surmising forbidden territory in her failure to volunteer the information. She was open to

Palmer. She didn't question his behavior, and she learned, through pointed questions, just as much about him as he did about her.

There were more Wednesdays after that, not many, but each one fuller than the last. And each time now, unlike the first, she looked up when he walked in the front door, a little smile of joy and relief on her lips. Palmer didn't count the weeks. All he cared about were the signs of progress, on the way to…what? He felt the truth like a surprise wrapped up in a brightly ribboned package, something to be saved for a special occasion with the expectation of good things inside.

Never did Elizabeth catch them together, but she knew. How could she not? His habits had changed, always home early Wednesday evenings, unlike his former self, frequently away. His habits in other ways had changed as well. Not the expected thing—a drawing away from Elizabeth—but the opposite, a renewed, passionate interest in her, something he genuinely felt, not an overcompensation driven by guilt and self-protection. He checked himself on that. His first worry had been that, yes, he felt the slightest bit sneaky (for which there was no reasonable explanation!), and perhaps his attention to Elizabeth was spurred by moral compulsion. But if that was the case, why was he enjoying himself so much?

He listened, rapt, to every small lament, every news item, every household instruction from Elizabeth. Their lovemaking increased. Elizabeth responded, noticeably pleased by his attention.

And then the night came when he turned on the bedside light. He wanted to see her face, wanted to watch every step in the progression of her desire, his focus intense, his need to know fierce—was it real? This unity he felt with Elizabeth—with everyone and everything!—atomized his corporal being, dispersed and wove the particles into his surroundings and thoughts. In the soft light he saw Elizabeth's face and thought of Maruta's (and Caitlin's?) and Maruta's again, now fading, driven away in his quest for the source of Elizabeth's pleasure, finding it in her comfortable features, the color rising in her cheeks. And there it was! That look he'd seen the first day, her gaze pressed into the back of Vadin's neck.

But it didn't upset him. He begrudged her nothing, reveled in her pleasure. He fell to her side and turned off the light, satisfied and happier than he'd ever been.

Side by side in the dark, they held hands, her right leg overlapping his left. "I forgot to tell you," she said. "Vaughn and Alice invited us to Sunday brunch the twenty-eighth. Michelle will be there, and we're supposed to somehow very casually get her to agree to show you her poetry." She laughed at the little joke in this.

Palmer smiled into the haze. How perfect! What else should two lovers do afterward but come down to earth and talk about the mundane events of the day? He expected nothing more, wanted nothing more from Elizabeth. How perfect life was!

During these weeks, nothing could deflate Palmer's high, not even the one small thought that played like a sour note in the back of his mind.

Time and again, like never before, he opened his address book to his daughter's cell number (he hadn't memorized or programmed it) and reached for the phone with every intention of calling her at college. But then he would think that maybe she was in the middle of class, or he would be distracted by some item of everyday business that crossed his mind, and he would retract his hand. Yet, he didn't perceive failure and blithely went on his way. There was no rush. He could always give Caitlin a ring tomorrow.

On the Wednesday before the Sunday brunch, Palmer followed his new pattern. He was higher than ever, the feeling of promise and possibility soaring as he stepped in the door and she looked up and smiled. Reasons hadn't been considered. Plans hadn't been made. He only knew that he wanted to sit next to her on the couch and have one of their intimate talks, feeling the electricity of her interest in him. It felt like the day to untie the ribbon, to play with the possibility of opening his special package, peeking inside, prolonging the excitement of anticipation.

By then, they'd talked about nearly everything, from work, to play, to love. So young, but so wise! She would discuss his work with him like a colleague. That day, she'd brought along one of his articles, folded up neatly on her lap, atop the piano books. A slippery, glossy piece of newsprint from the Sunday travel section, its elusiveness the cause of his downfall. If she hadn't brought it, well, what then? Would he have been spared?

She started to ask him about the article and leaned forward. The newspaper slipped off her lap onto the floor in front of her school-girl feet, the white ankle socks in brown penny loafers. She said, "Oh!," the last thing he would ever hear from her mouth, and put her hand on his shoulder—her first and last touch—as she leaned toward the floor. The touch felt like home, a place he didn't want to leave, yet as natural as it seemed, he discouraged her as he knew he must.

"No," he said, "let me get it," knowing and fearing that she would remove her hand, and she did. He bent forward to get the paper, a bit out of reach, and somehow he slipped to the floor, just slid off the edge of the couch in an awkward middle-aged way, his left thigh on the floor, his right hand on her bare knee to steady himself, his eyes level with the edge of her plaid skirt.

He didn't rise immediately, his ear caught by a dissonant sound, a glaring mistake, so uncharacteristic of Vadin, so unexpected that it delivered the shock of pain and offense. In his confusion, feeling the warmth of Maruta's knee and the relief of Vadin's flawless return to harmony, Palmer's head shot away from the studio toward the foyer.

And there they stood, filling the doorway with all the permanence and mystery of Egyptian pyramids. Genesis unknown, immaculate arrival. Beautiful people with beautiful offspring, the mother and the father (of course there was a father!), tall and fit with keen eyes.

Palmer picked up the newspaper and stood at once, patting Maruta's shoulder in a way meant to reassure both of them, perceived another way by the witnesses.

"Maruta," said the father quietly, his meaning clear.

She stood immediately and went to him, all the joy gone.

"We wanted to speak with Elizabeth," started the

mother in her everyday voice, but then she looked Palmer in the eye, saw something despicable, and shook her head. "I'll get Vadin."

The lesson wasn't over, Vadin still playing. The mother strode to the studio door, yanked it open, and halted Vadin mid-phrase, while the father put his arm around Maruta's shoulder and pulled her close to his side, leveling a stony look at Palmer. Maruta stared at the floor, looking very much, all of a sudden, like a normal teenager. The next moment they all whisked out of the house, and Elizabeth was in the living room, standing before him with accusation and puzzlement in her eyes.

"He'll never come back now," she said quietly, shaking her head, pursing her lips. "You've ruined this for me. Ruined everything."

Later that evening the police came to arrest him. "Sexual abuse," the complaint said, naming two instances, two consecutive Wednesdays, a puzzle to him until he remembered what had happened the week before. An innocent game! He'd commented on the beauty of her long, thick hair, and she'd challenged him, playfully, to style it. Sitting on the couch, her back to him, he'd braided and unbraided her hair, using his fingers as a comb. There'd been no tangles, only smoothness gliding through his fingers like the soft current of flowing water. Afterward, they'd laughed at his efforts. All a game is how it seemed to Palmer then.

By Friday, he was released on bail. Elizabeth came to pick him up at the courthouse, and they drove home in silence. Humiliated, Palmer had called her from a payphone in the lobby. He'd looked for her in the courtroom during his arraignment and bail hearing, but the only recognizable faces were those of Maruta's parents, the mother and the father.

Listening to the judge reading the charges against him, Palmer envisioned the scenario: Maruta's innocent, factual explanations twisted and reinterpreted by her parents and the police. She wasn't to blame in any of this, he was sure of it.

Elizabeth didn't speak to him for a day, avoided him in the house. Her manner wasn't punitive or angry or even cold. Simply indifferent, as if he were invisible. After their closeness of the previous weeks, her sudden withdrawal and lack of support sent him into a tailspin. By Saturday, his emotions were out of control. He cut her off in the hallway, pushed his hands into the wall on either side of her to block her escape, and demanded to know what she was thinking, accusing her of little faith and unjust punishment. "How can you possibly believe these people? How can you think I had any"—he could hardly utter the word—"*interest* in that girl?" Still, even as he said it, he doubted himself, knowing of his interest yet uncertain of its source and nature.

"I don't know what to think," she said, looking like a caged animal. Her eyes darted around the sides of his feet and in the spaces under his arms where they came out at right angles to the wall, boxing her in. Finally, she had nowhere to look but in his eyes, and he saw it then—her own guilt. She'd been discovered.

"You know exactly how it went, don't you?" he asked.

"Yes," she said.

"It's *not* what they say it is."

"Yes."

"Not that at all—"

"No. Not exactly that. I understand," she admitted.

"Not just the girl. You and the boy—"

"No!"

"But—"

"The boy? No, but I understand what you mean. It's a bigger thing."

"Yes."

"And what they're saying is a part of it."

He didn't respond.

"It is a part of it, isn't it?" she demanded.

"I didn't do those things!"

"I know that, Palmer. Don't you think I know that? Thoughts aren't crimes. Emotions aren't crimes. Attractions, even regrets…"

"Regrets?"

"Not crimes either."

Exposed, he couldn't look at her. He dropped his hands from the wall and freed her, giving her the choice. A moment later, she pulled him into her arms and they cried together.

That night they pretended at normalcy, and the next morning, although their hearts weren't in it, they planned to keep their date with Alice and Vaughn. Most likely their friends were unaware of Palmer's arrest, which had only made a small blurb in a local newspaper.

For the first time, Palmer felt the need to define his

relationship with these people. While he'd always considered them "good" friends, even "close" friends, the thought of revealing his current troubles seemed out of the question, nor could he fathom how he would get through the afternoon without giving himself away.

"Let's call and make an excuse," said Elizabeth, just as the phone rang. Palmer reached for it. "Vaughn. We were just about to—"

"About on your way over?"

"Well, not just yet," he stalled.

"Because I think we should, under the circumstances, call it off for today."

"All right. Fine, then. Michelle's not up for it?"

Silence. "Not up for it?" Vaughn snorted. "What was that you said? *'Bring her to me.'* Man, you have a problem." He ended their connection with a "click," and Palmer never heard from him again.

Through all of it, Palmer saw her face and couldn't erase the striking impression she'd made on him that first day. He had faith in her, still a little girl, but strong enough to speak her mind and compassionate enough to fight for him.

And she did, and the criminal charges, magically, were dropped. No apologies, no explanations. He thought of legal action, a suit for false arrest, but he didn't have it in him and wanted an end to things. The damage had already been done. Three weeks of torment had passed, a half-life of pain and mending yet ahead. A mixed blessing had come of it, a new closeness with Elizabeth, yet for all its goodness and comfort, their relationship was suddenly devoid of passion.

Once the criminal complaint was dismissed, his thoughts of Maruta disappeared, replaced with thoughts of Caitlin. He decided to call, not sure of what he would say, but he waited until a time when he felt in control of his voice and emotions.

She answered on the first ring, as if she hadn't looked at the display and was expecting an important call, a boyfriend perhaps.

"Oh, it's you, Daddy? How is everything?"

He could tell from those few words that she didn't know. And despite the hint of disappointment in her voice, she was glad to hear from him. He pictured her sitting at the desk in her sunny dorm room, her young face a rare combination of features that made her entirely new, never a reminder of Irene or himself.

"I'm fine," he said, but already his voice started to crack. He hadn't counted on this happening. He'd thought himself strong enough, and now he struggled for the command and self-possession he'd always taken for granted, finally accepting the truth in what lay underneath.

"It's been a long time," he managed to say, tears welling in his eyes. "Caitlin… Oh, Caitlin, I've been…" *such a bad father to you!* He stopped himself, finding the courage not to beg for her pity.

≈ROAD

LAINEY'S EYES POPPED open on impact. Her head bounced against the glass, something huge and black on the other side covering half the windshield before it flew over top. Instantaneous. Gone.

Green floored the brake, not letting up until the dust settled through the beam of the headlights. Lainey was certainly awake then, but not completely there. A warm drip trickled down her forehead, hung over the cavern of her eye socket and dropped to her cheek.

"He's dead." Green looked over his shoulder out the back window. "Christ! Where'd he go? He's dead for sure. No way anyone could've..." He shook his head, unbuckled his seatbelt with shaky hands, and started to open the door. In afterthought, he stopped and turned to her. "You okay?"

Lifting her hand slowly, Lainey probed the wet spot with numb fingertips. Her head throbbed—from this, or maybe from everything before. Through the spread of her fingers she saw the glass spiderweb, blinked and remembered the eyes meeting hers at the pane. She made a sound, apparently enough to satisfy Green. He was out the door, the headlights still on because everything was pitch, like God had bathed the world in tar.

She heard him outside, first pacing the road, then thrashing around in the bushes near their car—his car—a boring gray sedan, so perfect and recent, now with a webbed windowpane. "Christ! Where are you, man? I can't see a thing…" He rattled on continuously under moral compulsion, not waiting for an answer that wouldn't come.

She pulled at her door handle and shouldered her way out, unencumbered by the seatbelt she never wore but slowed from the weight of a stuporous shame.

"You out there? Give me a sign, anything…"

"Quiet," said Lainey.

"Can't see a damn thing—"

"Shut up!"

Green stopped cold in front of the car near the encroaching woods. Suddenly, Lainey was thinking entirely too clearly for her liking. She saw, better than Green, the illogic of his position. Disoriented, he was searching in the wrong place.

She saw his eyes in the headlights, remembering when he'd given her the same look earlier that evening. When earlier? Hours ago. That look of surprise and disgust. At the time, she'd snickered inwardly to suppress the possibility of regret. Now it didn't seem so funny.

"Listen," she commanded, sinking into a standing sit against the car.

They lapsed into silence and heard what had hummed all along in the background of Green's noise and her pulsing eyes. The engine. The motorcycle engine was still running but far behind them, around the bend of the curve.

"Christ! He's way back there—"

"Cut it with the 'Christ.'" She smirked, but it was too dark for him to see. Green's lack of imagination—even in his "naughty" words—had again opened him to Lainey's disdain, an impulse she'd easily displayed early in the evening when her sloshing mirth had the power to shock and surprise. Now, her satisfaction in it was gone.

Hardened against her, Green ignored Lainey and crossed the road, walking back along the blacktop. She remained propped against the passenger side of the car as she wiped away another drip with an index finger and glanced around. The sedan had come to rest on the gravely shoulder of this mountain road, bordered by a dense wood that swelled and receded before her eyes more rapidly than active surf. She turned halfway back, placing a hand on the car to steady herself. Green had already disappeared around the bend in the road.

The keys were still in the ignition—she could run— but instead she pushed away from the car, staggered around back and into the road to follow Green. With the headlights behind her and darkness in front, she thought she saw the white line, but maybe it was just a reflection on an oil slick. Reflection from what? Mountains were dark, to be sure, but there must be things like stars and a moon, natural light to guide her. She looked up and saw the promise of moonlight behind cloud cover, then leveled her cat eyes at the road ahead, making out its contour. Walking toward the bend, reeling a bit, she blinked and frowned against the pain.

Green was silent now, or too far ahead to be heard. Just the engine buzzing, wheels spinning. Now she almost wished she could hear him: "Christ" this and "Christ" that, not screaming, but with monotone panic like the insane.

She'd never seen him so excited. "Finally, the event of your life, Green," she said out loud to the dark night, imagining the return of an echo. Pacing, panicking, and babbling at roadside: how bad did he look anyway? Excited, that's all, not drunk. At least, not drunk enough to have caused *this*. He'd only had two (or was it three?) beers, the second and third foreign to him, downed with Lainey's encouragement through his puppy dog smile. It was the same smile he'd worn months ago, the day she dubbed him "Green" after the color of his favorite shirt. So she explained it, while secretly harboring a private joke about the real meaning behind the name.

He'd been her first sincere effort at respectability. "Dave and Elaine" would have matched the effort. But "Green and Lainey" helped just a little and gave her something quirky to hang onto when she was feeling nothing else. For eight months she'd put in the effort, unaware that the real Lainey had been planning sabotage from the start.

Around the bend, still no Green. She heard the click of her heels, crazy high heels in the mountains. She'd packed her sneakers in an overnight bag just in case he succeeded in dragging her out of the inn to some goddamn mountain trail. Click click click on cool asphalt, air too crisp on skin accustomed to lowland summer nights, click click click until she halted against the silence, suddenly awakening to the moment. The rumble was gone, the motorcycle engine had stopped. The silence triggered a flashback in a burst of sparks: male eyes through the windshield on impact. A man belonged to that motorcycle, and he was out there in the dark, bleeding and silent.

"You okay? Wake up, man, Christ, wake up!" Green was off the pavement a short distance ahead, on the side of the road opposite the side they'd been traveling. Lainey clicked toward his desperate sound onto the gravel of the shoulder, nearly stumbling on the black hulk of the motorcycle, which lay halfway into the bushes.

"Green? Where the hell are you?"

"Over here." She still couldn't see him but heard his voice coming from a clearing behind three feet of growth. "Christ, Lainey, this doesn't look good. He's dead. I knew it. He's dead." Green popped up like a jack-in-the-box, his silhouette, head to waist, now visible to her above the bushes.

She hesitated. He didn't move. As seconds ticked, the air lightened around them and she looked up. The clouds were dissipating. She looked at Green again, both of them silent, waiting for a sound. None came.

"How do you know?"

"I don't know. I just know. He's not moving. I tried to feel his breath or a pulse."

Nothing to do but push through it, twigs and burrs pulling at her cotton dress. On the other side of the bushes she stumbled on something and instinctively reached for Green's arm. He steadied her and let go. She looked down and confirmed that she hadn't stepped on the motorcyclist, who lay several feet away, his head closest to her.

The twisted black form didn't seem to bear any resemblance to humanity, but she wasn't afraid. Death wasn't something new to her and she gazed for a long time, remembering. A fellow partygoer, slumped over in a corner of a back room, needle in arm. And another time, an acquaintance splayed on concrete, five floors below her window of escape.

In the midst of Lainey's study, she suddenly preferred to look at Green. His eyes were almost visible now in the gray moonlight. A furrowed, glistening brow. He was sweating in this chill. She shuddered, almost wishing she still had the right to ask him to hold her. "What do we do?" she asked.

"Christ, Lainey, how do I know? We shouldn't even be here. It's three in the morning. We should be back at the inn, enjoying ourselves. We should be in bed, you know what I mean, Lainey—why did you have to do this to me way out here? I shouldn't even be on this road in the middle of the night, and now we need help and no one's around! I haven't seen a car for over an hour."

"Someone will come along—"

"How do you know? You've been passed out since I dragged you to the car."

"Sleeping, not passed out."

"Out of it, Lainey. Completely out of it."

She tried to muster her indignation again. Couldn't. He was right, of course, his caution no longer laughable but sane. She tried to remember exactly how "out of it" she'd been, an impossible exercise. This afternoon there'd been his fatigue from the drive and his insistence that they *nap* before dinner, a real nap like old people. She'd laughed and tucked him in and said she just had to get out and explore. The "town" wasn't much, a mountain hamlet with only the inn, a gas station, a general store and, yes, a bar, one of those rustic log cabin types with the neon beer sign in the window.

There was no reason to hesitate. A whole year had passed, and she was ready for the next step, the ultimate proof of her control. She entered the bar, dark and smoky. No rugged mountain men with dirty beards and yellow teeth, just a few city-looking people, tourists, like herself, everything still respectable. She would have just one.

She asked for her old favorite, gin, dressed up as a martini—a little too chic for this place, but the bartender returned with a frosty glass. After that, a second seemed fine, and then—she forgot—there was another and perhaps a fourth. She remembered the ladies' room and the comfort of her past ritual, the tooth brushing, mouth washing, perfume spritzing, wondering vaguely why these items still deserved permanent residence in her purse, now, after a year.

Back at the inn after nap time, he knew, he could tell of course, but he still thought it was cute, his sweetie having "a" drink in the bar while he slept. Dinnertime at the inn, cocktails before, his single beer, a martini for her, something he hadn't ever seen her do in their eight months together, but all part of the fun, sophisticated almost.

He sat three feet away on the other side of their

small table, erect and square, hair combed, closely shaved, prosperous, concerned, intelligent. Cautious. So cautious against the old Lainey emerging with all her arrogance at having lived, *really lived* through experiences he couldn't hope to imagine. Laughing and more drinks, her egging him on, another beer for him, and… When had it turned ugly?

After the fun part, she recalled only a few things, fleeting looks of disdain and repulsion on the faces of other patrons, Green's hand gripping her arm, his mouth forming the word "mistake" over and over again. Whose mistake? Hers, surely, but she remembered him claiming it as his own. His mistake in bringing her. His mistake in allowing this to happen. An acceptance of responsibility.

Like his panicky search near the car, completely wrong, backward, illogical—or was it? She remembered his look. The shock and disgust, but something more in his eyes, the significant thing. Recognition. He knew this wasn't an isolated incident. He knew who she was. His mistake had been in allowing himself to get this far with her.

And now, whose mistake was *this*? thought Lainey, looking down at the body.

"I shouldn't be talking," said Green, dropping his head. "I was drinking too. But I knew it and I was trying so hard. I stopped for coffee, you were knocked out in the car, so I stopped for a half hour at least and drank two cups of coffee. I was awake, I was mad really, so mad at you, Lainey. Why did you…?" He shook his head.

"Go on. I can take it."

"Just when everything was going good. Why did you

have to ruin it? Why?"

The question hung in the black space between them. Finally, Lainey said, "You shouldn't be so hard on yourself. You didn't drink much. Just a couple of beers."

"Three."

"Just three beers, that's nothing."

"Nothing to you."

"Not enough to make you drunk. I mean, who crossed the line anyway? It can't be your fault."

"I don't know. I really don't know. I was trying so hard. I was alert. I wasn't speeding and I was concentrating hard because the road is so dark, and then there's a curve and the headlight came at me. I can't say whose fault it was, but what does it matter? We have to get help. I tried my cell—it's a dead zone, no coverage. There's a town about ten miles ahead. The car's okay, just a few dents and the broken windshield. I can hang out the window to see the road."

"Okay, let's go," said Lainey.

"Wait a minute. You stay here in case someone drives by."

"But there haven't been any cars—"

"You have to stay. If we both leave and they see us on the road before we get help, they'll accuse us of running, no matter what we say."

"Then I'll go and you stay."

He hesitated and she knew why. He didn't trust her to get help. "You're drunk," he said. "I won't let you drive my car."

"I'm sober now."

"You should see yourself. It hasn't been that long.

And your head too, it's bleeding."

"Don't leave me here with a corpse. We're both going. He's dead. It doesn't matter. Why do we need help anyway? You're okay, I'm okay—"

"I don't run from things, Lainey. I don't run and hide. That's not my style." He was calm now, sure about what he had to do. He backed off, threw his leg over the bushes, tore loose of the thorns, and righted himself on the shoulder. "Don't make me beg. You owe me this much. Just stay here with him, and when I come back, we'll both tell them the truth. Will you do that much?" He stood tall and waited, the whole of him a magnificent dark pearl in the spreading moonlight.

She said nothing, swaying in the clean air, not moving toward Green or away from the body. Yes, she thought, I'll do that much, and Green paused to catch her thought before backing up a step or two, turning, walking toward his car, disappearing behind the curve.

Not looking down, she inched away from the body, considering where, exactly, to wait. Closer to the road so she could stop any car that might pass. She heard Green's car starting up, slipping away over the crunch of gravel. She shivered under the thin cotton, angry to have let him leave her here without a sweater at least.

Hesitating, not enjoying the thought of another climb through the bushes, she glanced down and sideways at the motorcyclist, now bathed in moonlight. His face glistened with blood, and she could make out his features, the nose, eyelids, and mouth still perfectly formed, not mashed the way she'd expected. Hair wet and matted in spots. No helmet.

Why did you have to do it, Lainey? spoke the blood-ied lips. Why did you have to ruin it when everything was going so well? Everything so perfect, too perfect and tidy, in place, controlled, on schedule, routine, sunny, pleasant, mild and sweet, good, such a good man who liked you, maybe loved you in his cautious way, warm and secure. Why did you have to ruin that?

"Live or die," she said out loud to the corpse, remembering the feel of wind on her face and bare head, whipping her hair, arms encircling a leather barrel chest as they leaned into a curve, on the razor edge between recovery and destruction. "Live or die, there's nothing in between," she declared, gazing into his lifeless face. "Dave Green didn't do this at thirty miles an hour with his seatbelt on. Don't tell me you weren't blasting around that curve, looking to fly."

"No," said the body.

"Don't tell me—"

"No."

Lainey dropped to her knees, next to his head. She touched his lips. They were warm. She touched his hand. It was cold. "No," he said again, and she saw his lips move.

"We're getting help," she said. "We're getting help. Someone will be here."

"No."

She touched his hand again, tried to hold it, but the fingers were limp, the muscles apparently useless. "Do you feel this?" she asked. "Do you feel me touching your hand?"

"No." His eyes fluttered open and he stared up at

her, whether seeing or responding to her, she couldn't tell.

Tears sprang to her eyes and mucus thickened her throat. You poor bastard, she thought but wouldn't say, not to a survivor who would never live again, whichever way it went. Live or die doesn't always work, does it, my friend? Sometimes you just end up somewhere in-between, crippled.

And she held his hand in hers, then cupped their two hands in her palm, and waited with him until the ambulance came for them both.

⩘SIGNIFICANT DETAILS

ABBY WHALEN OPENED her notebook and looked at her watch. "3:15 p.m., Mrs. Murphy, mailbox (usual*)," she scribbled in pencil.

"Usual" meant the way Mrs. Murphy, driving her new, 1990 blue Pontiac station wagon (5TW 467), would scrape the curb on the wrong side of the street as she sidled up to her mailbox, needing to shift between D and R several times to get just close enough. Her kids would be fighting in the back seat. She would hit the window button and extend an arm into the box, her double chin jiggling and lengthening as she craned to see if she'd gotten every last item of junk mail. The asterisk meant that Abby had written it all before in one of her many spiral notebooks.

Mrs. Murphy always came home about this time after picking up her children from the middle school, just five blocks away. In sixth and eighth grades they were, a girl and a boy, Mrs. Murphy's pudgy clones, her back-seat prisoners.

Stacie wasn't like those children. Didn't take the school bus and never allowed herself to be driven even though, in the old neighborhood, their house had been at least a half mile from the high school. Stacie always walked, lean and strong, her face full of sunshine.

Abby looked at her watch again. Still 3:15. Now 3:16. Nearly every day it was about this time, as if the middle school administration and Mrs. Murphy had conspired against her. But then, she reminded herself, the time had never been established with certainty. She rarely wore a watch in those days.

Probably she'd said "about" or "around." Whatever the reason, the time stuck in his head and was repeated throughout, magnifying its importance.

"And what happened at about 3:15 on the afternoon of May 20th, Mrs. Whalen?" Funny how lawyers start so many sentences with "and." The habit annoyed Abby, undercutting her reverence for this tall young man with a righteous air, exposing her need to extract every ounce of illusory protection he afforded.

"Well," she answered, feeling the heat of twelve pairs of eyes, "Stacie went to visit Andrea Benson, a friend who lived a few blocks away. She said she would be back by dinner, and she left."

"And what did you do then?"

I ran to the door and called her back, screamed Abby, her throat becoming thick before she said, "I looked out the window as she went down our front walk. I waved goodbye…"

"And?"

"And…she didn't see me. Then the phone was ringing, and I turned away from the window."

* * *

They—or rather Abby—had chosen this house for its windows. Four big, bay windows on the ground floor, two in the living room and two in the dining room, large windows and a sliding glass door in the kitchen. George might not have wanted it that way, but he quietly followed, sensing Abby's need, knowing without conscious awareness that the move was the first step in their silent, joint project to grind down the cutting blade of their pain, until it could inflict only a dull ache.

Other people might have reacted differently, might have wanted to close themselves in. But for Abby and George, it was enough to run from the old neighborhood and come to a new place as virtual unknowns—that youngish retired couple. Neighbors surrounded their square, half-acre lot, giving it a different feeling from the old house where their backyard—and all the backyards on their side of the street—bordered a heavily wooded county park. A plus for their growing girl, they had thought, a place for her to commune with nature, to explore and discover.

In the new house, Abby kept her windows uncovered, the curtains like tight accordions at their edges, allowing everything in. Not much concerned about what the neighbors thought, she still felt a small sense of relief that they usually didn't notice her in the corner of one window or another. When someone happened to look her way, she would pick up one of the many framed photographs clogging the sills, dust and replace it.

That's one thing about people: most of the time they just go about their own business, oblivious to anything beyond their own noses. She knew. She had been that way herself.

"And when did the defendant, Earl Diggins, move into the house next door?"

"Just a couple of months before…it happened."

"Did you have any contact with the defendant following his move next door?"

"Well, a couple of days after he moved in, I was on the front walk with Stacie when he came out of his house. We introduced ourselves and chatted, but there was something so strange about—"

"Objection."

"Sustained. Mrs. Whalen, just tell us what happened. No opinions, please." The judge delivered these instructions in a gentle voice reserved just for her.

"Okay. Mr. Diggins was looking at my daughter while I talked to him, not looking at me but at her, even though she wasn't saying anything."

"In the weeks that followed, did the defendant have any contact with your daughter?"

"Many times. You see, she always walked past his house to go to school and on her way to her friends' houses, and she told me—"

"Objection!"

"Sustained. Mrs. Whalen, did you personally see Mr. Diggins with your daughter? Just tell us what you saw."

"I, well, there was only once, because I didn't follow her around. She was sixteen and nearly grown, you see…"

"I understand." The judge was kind. "Please tell us about the time you saw them together."

"It was about three weeks after he moved in. I happened to look out the window as my daughter was walking home around dinnertime. He was near the sidewalk in front of his house, wearing a business suit like he'd just come home from work. He greeted my daughter and started to talk to her. They talked for maybe a few minutes and she came on home."

"Could you hear the conversation?"

"No. I was in the house. But he was looking at her again in that strange way."

"Objection."

"Sustained. Please disregard that last statement, members of the jury."

Her notes became shorter as she came to know her neighbors' daily routines. A flurry of activity between 7:00 and 8:30 in the morning as people drove off to work and children walked (or were driven) to school. The rest of the day, until the schools let out, was spotty. Then came the evening commuters. In between, Abby did the housework and cooking, often keeping a bay window within her peripheral vision, her eye catching any flicker of movement. Some things she could do while seated at a window: reading, sewing, knitting for her nephew's baby.

George fit his routine around Abby's. He had retired at the age of sixty-two following a year of misery, frequent absence, failing concentration, and suspicion of his own uselessness. Nothing he'd tried had helped, a lighter workload, a change of assignment, or his move with Abby to the new neighborhood. Not knowing what he might do any better for the next twenty or thirty years, he accepted an early retirement plan, coming home to an easy chair he didn't need.

That first year at home, Abby had saved him with her mechanical form of survival. She got up with the alarm every morning and designed the structure of their lives. They spoke little, their looks and touches rarely breaking through their separate spheres, but Abby's movement through the tasks of daily life and her silent expectation of his participation were all he needed to stay among the living.

With time, George awakened to the world. Now, at sixty-four, he was determined to overcome the weight of retirement, not allowing it to augment his pain. He did all the errands and shopping (Abby rarely made it out) and volunteered occasional afternoons at the community center. Lately, he'd been spending hours in his basement workshop on a project he was not yet prepared to reveal. "What's keeping you so busy down there?" Abby asked absentmindedly while staring out a window. "I'm making something," he told her, knowing she wouldn't go looking. "I'll show you when it's done."

Jogging was the newest part of his routine, mid-morning after his breakfast settled. The length of his route gradually increased as his strength returned. The even rhythms of his plodding feet, his breath, his beating heart, all tugged at the dormant life within, pulling out the quality that had once, long ago, shone with an irresistible sparkle in his gray eyes.

Now, at mealtimes, he would touch Abby's hand or kiss her cheek before leaving the table. His touch begged a response. She would look at him directly or turn her head with a wistful smile.

One spring morning he lightly caressed her hand as it lay on the table. She smiled at him, then turned to the window, looking beyond their daughter on the windowsill—dozens of pairs of eyes, all hers—for once not interested in the neighbors as she gazed out into their own front yard. "Aren't the cherry blossoms lovely?" she said, releasing a small explosion of joy in his heart.

"That evening, when Stacie failed to return by dinnertime, what did you do?"

"At six-thirty I called the Benson residence. Andrea said that Stacie had left for home about an hour ago."

"What did you do then?"

"I walked to the Bensons' house and back again, taking the streets I thought she might have taken."

"Did you walk past the defendant's residence?"

"Yes. On my way back, I paused in front of his house for a long time."

"Why?"

"Objection."

Because he'd been driving home when he saw her leave the Bensons' house, and he stopped and offered her a ride, and she accepted out of politeness because he wasn't really a stranger, but instead of dropping her home he drove straight into his own driveway, distracting her with pleasant conversation as he clicked the garage door opener and drove inside before she had time to think…

"Sustained. Please disregard the last question, Mrs. Whalen."

"What did you observe when you paused in front of

the defendant's house?"

"I observed that his garage door was closed, the curtains were shut, and a single light, a dim light, was on in the living room. I couldn't see anyone inside. I debated whether to ring the bell…"

"Please stick to your observations and actions," instructed the judge.

"Yes, well, I didn't observe much else."

"How long did you stand there?"

"At least ten minutes."

"And what did you do then?"

"I went home and called the police."

Dusting and rearranging took a good deal of her time. Abby had started with the idea of picking one photograph for each year of her daughter's life, but the number quickly swelled as she sorted through albums and boxes of old photographs, always finding another that had to be included. For every photo she picked, George purchased or made a frame for it in his workroom. Of every shape and size, the frames were chosen with care from the best quality materials: silver, crystal, brass, tapestry, porcelain, mahogany.

The pictures were the finest of the lot. Still, none of them did her justice. The two-dimensional images failed to capture Stacie's essence, the quality that had drawn people to her: a comfortable self-confidence grown from infinite parental love, melting without boundary into her natural love for others. Her smile included everyone within its breadth.

Stacie had been a miracle baby, arriving twelve years

into their marriage, well after all hopes for babies had faded. Abby, forty, George, forty-five, parents for the first time. In the seventh month of her pregnancy, Abby quit her secretarial job to devote her life to her child. Abby and George pampered and worried, cooed and caressed their little one. Despite the abundance of attention they bestowed, Stacie evolved without a trace of conceit or selfishness, her curiosity and enthusiasm for life and all living things overcoming any thought of self.

Like a caricature of first-time parents, Abby and George were never without a camera close at hand, snapping shots in quick succession. Now, Abby handled the static relics of those years, setting posed shots along-side candid ones, smiling pictures next to melancholy ones, categorizing them by age, moving and rearranging them into patterns, lines, or a hodgepodge, all in an effort to capture her spirit. Abby yearned for just one fleeting moment of belief in Stacie's existence and presence, yet failed to achieve even that.

Perhaps her distaste for the "and" habit grew because the other lawyer, the one she didn't want to like, also fell into it from time to time. He was outwardly pleasant enough with his slick smile and rehearsed sympathy for the grieving mother, but no more cordial, even less so, than his chumminess with the defendant. At the defense table he would lean into and touch and smile at Diggins, making her cringe involuntarily whenever he peeled him-self from his client to approach her, coming too close to the witness stand with the smell of blood on his hands.

"And you testified, did you not, that Stacie passed by

Mr. Diggins' house frequently?"

"Yes, I said that."

"And she usually wore earrings, correct?"

"Yes. Her ears were pierced."

"So she could have lost this earring, People's Exhibit One," he held it up, "on any of the days she passed Mr. Diggins' house, isn't that right?"

"No."

"No?"

"It was in his car the night she disappeared."

"You mean, in his car on the day of the search, a month later?"

"Well, I don't know…"

"No, I guess you don't. Stacie had several pairs of earrings, didn't she?"

"Yes."

"More than a dozen?"

"Yes."

"And would it be fair to say that she changed earrings frequently?"

"Well, yes."

"And isn't it also possible that she changed her earrings during the day, wearing one pair in the morning and one pair in the afternoon?"

"It's possible. Not likely. She was a busy girl."

"So busy some days that she might have forgotten to put on any earrings at all?"

"I doubt it. She seemed to have them on all the time."

"It seemed that way on May 20th?"

"Seemed what way?"

"That she wore earrings to Andrea's house."

"Yes. I saw her when she walked by the kitchen door at 3:15, on her way out."

"Briefly?"

"Yes, briefly."

"And it seemed to you that she wore earrings then?"

"She wore earrings."

"Your eyes were on her earrings when you briefly saw her?"

"Well, no. But I had seen her that morning."

"And your eyes were on her earrings then?"

"No, but those were her favorite earrings and I'm fairly certain she wore them."

"Fairly certain?"

"Yes."

The attorney paused, took a deep breath and grabbed her eyes with his own. She couldn't escape. "Mrs. Whalen, look deep in your heart and tell me if you are entirely certain, one hundred percent certain, that she wore those earrings that day."

Abby clutched the arms of the wooden chair, sitting on the edge between fact and intuition. Everyone waited.

"Well," she said, her voice nearly a whisper, "maybe not a hundred percent."

"And that's because, during those times you briefly saw her, it was just another ordinary day, wasn't it?"

"Yes."

"And, on an ordinary day, it wasn't significant which earrings she wore, isn't that right?"

She nodded and lowered her head. "But later, when I thought about it, I remembered—"

"Yes, later. It wasn't until a month later, was it? When the body was found and the detective told you of the search in Mr. Diggins' car. Isn't that the first time you thought of it and tried to remember?"

Abby wouldn't answer, her silence giving him the tacit agreement he needed.

When they moved, they discarded many of Stacie's possessions, keeping only the most precious things that spoke uniquely of her, the things Stacie never would have thrown away. Like the earrings. Abby battled the immediate urge to destroy them, especially the one returned by the district attorney's office—the symbol of Abby's inattentiveness and neglect. She laid it with the others in a small jewelry case which she tucked between two teddy bears in the box.

While packing, she inspected the earrings for the last time, touching them, counting them again. Fifteen pairs in all—and three singles, including People's Exhibit One, found wedged in the crevice of the front passenger seat in Diggins' car. Its mate was gone, not in Stacie's room, nowhere near or on what was left of Stacie, denying Abby the proof of her recollection. Diggins had destroyed it, of course.

But Abby puzzled over the other two singles, reviving her internal castigation. Stacie had, after all, lost earrings on other occasions without telling her mother. Details that Abby had missed. Something the defendant's lawyer had supposed and argued to the jury.

She examined People's Exhibit One for many minutes before laying it to rest. How could she really know for certain that Stacie had worn it that day? It was so very similar to all the others, a long, dangling earring, the kind that teens love, big and bright and multi-colored, pink and purple outlined in a triangle of shiny brass. It was large enough to reflect a ray of sunlight, to draw his eye to the curb where it lay as he drove out his driveway one morning, a few days before she was last seen.

That was the story he gave from the witness stand. He sat calmly in his gray business suit, not a line out of place, not a break in his voice, not a drop of perspiration on his brow. Almost too perfect. The earring caught his eye, he said, and he drove up slowly and opened his car door, leaned out, picked it up, and tossed it in the passenger seat. He thought it might be Stacie's and he would return it to her later, but he was late for work, and he continued on. It must have become wedged into the crevice of the seat, and so he completely forgot about it, until the police came knocking one day.

"And" then, the ultimate questions and answers. No, he hadn't seen Stacie on May 20th. No, he didn't do those things to her, things that weren't even within the realm of Stacie's curiosity and imagination, many of those things no more than intelligent guesses by the experts who examined her decomposed remains, found in a shallow grave in the county park, a month later. He had been clever and careful, his house vacuumed and scrubbed clean, the only oversight—the earring—easily explained. Nothing else. No clothing or skin or blood or tears.

Only Abby's. At least a year of daily and nightly tears, the bitterest spilled on the day of the verdict when Diggins, cool and calm with just the trace of a smile, walked from the courtroom, a free man.

Torrents of tears as she daily and nightly inhabited Stacie's room, touching and kissing her things, holding them to her heart, every last teddy bear, dress, shoe, and earring. The tears stung her puffy eyes and choked her throat until the day when Abby selected the most important possessions, packed them slowly with care, and finally turned her back on her little girl's bedroom. That was the day her tears ran out.

In the new house, Stacie's box resided in a little-used closet. Abby never opened it, and her eyes have been dry and emotionless now these two years.

One June morning, George's side of the bed was empty when Abby awoke. He had cracked the window open, allowing a slice of cool, fragrant air into the room.

Before she could move her aching limbs, he came in, opened the shades, and sat next to her on the bed. His eyes were bright and alive. "I woke up early and couldn't get back to sleep," he explained, taking her hand, looking for something in her eyes.

She sat up slowly and glanced at the radio alarm clock, her thoughts in half-dream. "It's Saturday? No, it's Friday, isn't it? I'd better get up. I'll be late."

"I'll get the breakfast," he said and left the room.

But their breakfast wasn't ready when she came into the kitchen. "Come," he said, his eyes brighter than before. He smiled at her puzzled expression and took her hand, leading her into the living room, stopping a few feet from the central bay window. "Happy anniversary," he said.

Abby gulped a small breath through her mouth and held it. George watched her eyes, looking for a change, but he saw only the tiniest flicker. He was taking a big risk, he knew, but it was a risk he had to take. He followed her eyes as they moved from the central bay window to the one on the side of the house, where she paused briefly before turning and tilting her head, peering through the passageway into the dining room, seeking out the bay window next to the dining room table.

Abby straightened, her gaze returning to the window directly in front. Her eyes glazed over, looking without seeing, then suddenly were shot with panic, darting from place to place in the room, finally coming to rest on the mantelpiece. There, alone, stood the single remaining photograph of Stacie, Abby's favorite, a candid close-up of her smiling teenage face. The wrinkle in Abby's brow relaxed, her concern not entirely gone. "The others?" she asked George, her eyes still glued to Stacie's photograph.

"Don't worry," he said. "I've just put them away. Temporarily."

Abby nodded slowly, trancelike, and turned her gaze to the windowsill again, ready at last to consider what George had done. She stepped forward, her eyes focusing. Still busy and clogged, the sill now held dozens of photographs of George and Abby. Their faces were dewy, or smiling, or wistfully happy. Two years of courtship, their wedding, twelve years before Stacie. All before Stacie.

"There's a lot here," she said quietly.

"Yes. There was a lot." He hesitated, afraid to say it, knowing he must. "I've never forgotten those years, even after everything else."

Abby nodded, as if accepting without agreeing. She picked up the most prominent photograph, an enlargement of a black-and-white snapshot taken by her sister the day they announced their engagement to the family. Sitting on the lawn, Abby leaned back into George's chest, his arm circling her shoulders in front. Knowledge of their own inevitable, natural unity lived in their features.

She outlined the figures with an index finger.

"Do you remember that day?" asked George.

She pulled the frame to her chest and buried it under her crossed arms. "Yes," she said, gazing into the past. She didn't need the photograph to remind her of the early spring lawn, the sweet breeze in her hair, and the love in her heart. She didn't need the photograph to recall her bright yellow sundress with a grass stain over her right knee, or the smell of George's warm forearm wrapped around her shoulders. It hadn't been just another ordinary day. Every detail resided deeply within her.

"Yes, I remember," she said, feeling the water flow into her eyes once again.

⨇MY CAR KNOWS WHERE I AM

THE GREEN IS expansive, grown from stolen water. I'm in an arid western state in a backyard in the sun at a barbeque with thirty or more people I don't know, eating grilled burgers. A single-parent family nibbles just beyond the fence, momma doe with two, white-spotted May offspring. The owners of this home—Joe and Jane?—are natives. Other mammals on the lawn are refugees.

We've been talking automotive. My car is the highly trumpeted Elecflick Ximus, completely rechargeable. At the moment, it may be floating somewhere in the San Bernardino Valley after the mega 9.5 pushed a forty-foot wave over the California coastline.

I was in the air at the time, six days ago, on my way to New York. The nonstops were all booked, and this one had a layover in Phoenix or Albuquerque or Salt Lake. I've forgotten. I disembarked and failed to catch the next leg. The deer no longer know their mountain, and I've developed an aversion for any coastline.

In peripheral vision now, they remain rigidly im-mobile. The deer, after all, are made of plaster.

"Take a look at this," says a woman I met five

minutes ago. A dribble of bloody juice escapes the side of her mouth. She doesn't seem to notice and I'm not inclined to point it out. The tanned fingers of her right hand are a vise around the soaked, Angus beef-filled bun, and the tanned fingers of her left clutch a greasy, indestructible plastic plate. This woman has a voracious attractiveness, owing to her enthusiastic consumption of beef and vehicle conversation.

She nudges me toward the driveway at the edge of the yard. "All I have to do is this," she says, nodding in the direction of a glaring candy-apple red sports coupe. Predictably, her nifty transport blinks and smiles with a little ripple of recognition along its body.

"Nice," I say, unimpressed. My car knows where I am.

"The implant was painless," she boasts, and takes another huge bite of chopped meat.

I look at her with a raised eyebrow and squeeze a dimple into my left cheek. When I'm driving Nilla and deliver this look through the side window, any woman in the next lane will respond. I'm feeling nostalgic for those long hours creeping on L.A. freeways, the women distant and contained in glass and chrome.

She doesn't have to put the burger down. With both hands fully loaded, she makes a motion with her head, tilting the crown toward me then up and away in an undulation like a cat stroking her owner's calf muscle, asking for a rub. At the end of her sultry motion, her pony-tailed head is tilted away with the side of her neck exposed to me, where I see it, just behind the ear. A fresh pink slit in the white where the sun can't reach. Lips might have begged to touch this delicate bit of skin, but it's been taken.

"How long to connect?" I ask, because it's expected.

"Instantaneous." Candy apple chirps in agreement.

A man within earshot burps, "yeah!" as if we are three instead of two. He's in cargo shorts, partially covered with a dangling polo, and his ejaculation has just caused him to drop a salsa-filled tortilla chip onto the lawn, splattering a little red on his lavender-cotton chest on the way down. "I was dating a chick had one of those," he says, looking at the woman and bouncing his head violently sideways in the direction of candy-apple coupe.

I pretend to regard it again. I'm not agog over red, preferring Nilla's pure white. She's fully self-cleaning, self-waxing, always immaculate upon entry. She's mine, chipless. These two couldn't know.

"Where is it?" I say.

"You mean, where is *she*?" The man is revved, excited about the little joke he's building up in his head.

I shrug. I got what I came for. My burger's been down for five minutes, I've survived another day, and I'm just waiting for my exit. She may come this time, she may not. There's always another barbeque on the next block.

"They ran off together. It was love. It was *that* intimate." He's got a self-loving grin on his sweaty face.

"Is this why you're talking to me?" asks the woman, winking at him.

I shrug again, so bored I can't even pretend to feel threatened enough to force a dimple. I'm ready to go find the sunset, survive another night without Nilla if I have to, and awake to a new day, a new barbeque.

But without warning, it feels like California again. The ground shakes, air and light are cut off, and my exit is snuffed before I can make the move. Our host and hostess, Joe and Jane, have arrived to see "how we all are doing." Between them, they easily weigh five hundred pounds, with a good three hundred of that on Joe. Soon, it becomes clear that the woman I'm with—she has a name, Dr. Peggy Carmichael—is Jane's gastroenterological surgeon. Profusely thanking the doctor, Jane is ecstatic to be fully recovered from her third gastric bypass, and she's been trying to convince her husband to give it a try.

They deferentially address her as "Dr. Carmichael," but she insists on "Peggy," and the three of them easily fall into cordial intimacy, having shared so many gastrointestinal experiences. While Jane is talking, Peggy takes two enormous, throat clogging bites, her eyes rolling. The man with the salsa splatter is transparently miffed at being overshadowed.

"I owe no," says Joe, mouth and plate loaded. This might have meant "I don't know."

Jane displays her comparatively diminutive burger. "Joe. See here, I'm up to eight ounces already. Next month it'll be twelve. You build up again, you'll see."

"That's the beauty of it," says the doctor.

Along with her happy chatter, Jane's eyes have been shifting, first toward salsa shirt, giving him an in-the-know smile, then toward me, with a quizzical, slightly disapproving cast under the affected pleasantness. "Peggy! I don't think we've been introduced to your friend."

"Forgive me," says Peggy, turning to me expectantly.

"No, forgive me," I say. "It's been a great party, but I must be off." I squeeze the doctor's elbow. "Sorry, Peggy, I forgot to tell you. A previous engagement."

"Never you mind now," she says with a little laugh, but candy apple senses otherwise and gives a tinny snarl.

I send Jane the dimple. "Thanks for the great food, and for, well…," and I'm walking off toward the driveway as Jane blurts, "You're welcome!" I glance back fleetingly, enough to catch the beginning of her wilting smile. I can imagine the rest of what takes place behind my back.

Now there will be talk.

I make my way past a small cluster of people hovering over their cars in the section of driveway nearest the backyard, then proceed along an endless string of vehicles parked the length of the drive and beyond, down half the cul-de-sac. As I pass, each vehicle speaks or reverbs or flashes or emits or regards me warily in silence. Finally, I'm away from the people and free of their lined-up metal. Out on a stretch of groomed asphalt with an empty-lawned mansion on either side, her voice comes to me. I can hear her again.

I'm coming. I know where you are. I will be there.

From the start, she's known how to adapt pitch and vibration to my needs. She embodies any mood, any moment. Her voice was once the sea. There were days and nights we spent together in Malibu, the sun over the water, followed by the moon, when she spoke to me in the sound of the waves, and that endless stretch was an opening to freedom, before it became a destructive force. Her voice was the lulling, stroking sound of motion without fear. But all of that has changed, and I cannot return.

I tell her I need a savior.

Her voice comes back, different, adapted. *Things have changed, but we will be the way we were.*

A noise disturbs our communication. Behind me, a black gorilla pants heavily in the sun, oozing oil and the fetid fumes of fossil fuels. Joe is one of the last stubborn holdouts, guzzled up and sucking on dinosaur bones. He will sacrifice his duodenum before he surrenders the petroleum for his SUV.

He stops next to me and leans out the window over a bent-elbow slab of lard, pretending at friendliness. "Geez guy, where'd you park?"

I shrug my shoulders, laugh, and swipe the air. It's all a joke.

"Need a ride?"

"No thanks." I keep walking, and silence returns for a while. But then I hear the rumble and growl. He pants up slowly from the rear and stops again.

"Can't get too far on foot now, can you?"

"Don't worry. Someone's coming for me." My defensive cheeriness is wearing thin, and now, even without looking at him, I can feel the heat of his smoldering resentment.

"Yeah, I've heard that one."

It seems he's chased after unknown guests before. Today I saw them, people like me, other refugees sprinkled on his lawn, melting in. His land is wide open, doesn't he see? An invitation. No walls, no megaphones, no firing squads.

I keep walking, and this time he holds back and doesn't come for a while, not until I arrive at an empty crossroads. I stand there, indecisive, looking right, looking left. This time when he comes up behind and stops, I turn toward him. The sun is at my back and in his face. He's above me, hanging out the window at the top of a massive black door, five breakfast sausages gripping the edge.

"Just what is it you want from us?" he demands.

He's a curious, clattering piece of flesh. His face is red, a continuous mound from shoulder to neck to ears to buzz cut, the hole in the middle surprisingly small, expandable, but now empty of food, allowing the tongue to wax very articulate.

"You come into my backyard and eat my food! D'ya think burgers grow on trees?"

I do not. I cast around but find no trees, only asphalt, lawns, and sprinkler systems for miles.

"Look at you. It gets worse every day! More of you coming here, overrunning the place."

Joe has smartened up. Jane, the more intuitive, recognized me immediately and said so to her husband on my way out, behind my back. Informed him of the threat I pose. *Go after him, Joe,* she commanded, and he dutifully worked himself up. He would protect his woman, his eight-ouncer. Pride was involved. Home and territory and diluted testosterone.

"What gives you the right?" he kept on. "You come here, don't know our ways, don't speak our language. You think I'm responsible for you?" The sausages fly off the window well in a frantic gesture. "Did I tell you where to be born, where to live?" He points over my head in the general direction of California. "Is it my fault what happened? Is it my fault they can't take care of you?"

My mind is elsewhere and my body numb. I'm not trying to gall him with silence. His noise is causing interference, cutting off transmission. I'm searching for the signal, my connection to Nilla. But I keep my eyes fixed to his two little pinholes squeezed in the flesh, a body quivering with raw emotion.

"I'll report you!" he dares. "I have to report you!"

I would be the first to agree that we don't speak the same language. His tongue is new to me, and I don't want to learn it.

In my parting, direct look into his eyes, I'm strong and confident, showing him the importance I still possess, enough to be needed and wanted elsewhere. I acknowledge him with a nod, one mammal to another, and choose a direction, turning left to walk west. The gesture is lost on him.

I'm on a broader road now, the one that links all the little cul-de-sacs like Joe's. The road is empty, the quiet is complete, my stomach is full, the late afternoon air is dry and temperate, 70 degrees. Birds and trees and lakes do not exist and have never existed in this place God intended as desert and man transformed into his spotless, death-negating composition. No moisture or leavings of nature mar these perfect streets.

I've forgotten him, but he has not forgotten me.

First, there is the sudden, big sound of his heavy right foot hitting the gas pedal, once, twice, three times, pumping a monstrous internal combustion of fuel, spark, and piston. It fights the left foot, firmly and heavily planted on the brake pedal.

Second, the left foot is released.

Third, a roar behind me...

Nilla appears a hundred yards ahead, the outline of her body, demure but distinct within a radiant aura of pure white. We share a frozen moment of recognition. I see her and know her in the split second before everything accelerates to the speed of light.

She rushes forward to save me.

∾GRAY ZONE

I DIDN'T NOTICE what went on between them until that September, a couple of months after *Proffitt v. Florida*, when death was again possible, intensely upon us. It was 1976. William Douglas Jones had just been sentenced under Florida's capital punishment law, found constitutional in *Proffitt*, and we were searching for mitigation, anything to convince an appellate court that Jones had been wrongly condemned to death.

The case weighed heavier than its two-thousand-page transcript, which Emma and I slogged through in chunks, the tissue-thin paper clinging to our sweaty fingertips. The heat was moist and the air thick with emerging personality—those secrets kept from me all the previous year.

Several recent setbacks for the Poverty Law Center added to our discomfort. My buffers, the older, more experienced attorneys, had left, Betty to care for her ailing father, and Keith to join a law firm. In the heat of August, our single, battered air conditioner in the communal office went down, and then, after Labor Day, our three summer interns in the anteroom went back to law school.

A little money could have fixed these shortcomings, but the federal grant had been cut and private contributions were down as the popular sentiment swung slightly in favor of public execution, now that the Supreme Court had called an end to the moratorium.

Keith and Betty's absence should have given us more air to breathe in our shared space, but oddly enough, the extra room closed us in on one another. Emma and I, our tension, expanded into the vacancy, and what little remained was filled by increasing visits from Blake Adamson, our executive director. Wearing such an impressive title at the tender age of thirty-four, Blake worked at fostering a dual image of colleague and authority figure to Emma and me, both twenty-seven and only a few years out of law school. The mixture was imprecise and fed my transient bouts of insecurity despite the congenial looseness of our tight-knit group.

Blake would spring unexpectedly from his tiny private office, the door opening directly into our room, just poking his nose in or staying a while, mostly to hover over Emma. At first, I took these extra visits as a sign of his anxiety about the diminishing ranks and our inability to move through the stacks of waiting appeals. We were forced to concentrate on one case at a time, whichever presented the most compelling crisis. That September it was William Douglas Jones.

Our office, Emma's and mine, was a square room not much bigger than my Park Avenue office is today, crammed with four child-size desks. Each of three walls held a desk, and the fourth wall was cut in half by Blake's door, sandwiched by file cabinets. The fourth desk, mine, was plunked exactly in the middle of the room. No other place for it. Emma was on the wall to my left.

At the time, I never paused to consider why I didn't switch to one of the vacant desks when our two colleagues resigned. Now I understand. Emma, Keith, and Betty all sat facing their respective walls, but I sat in the middle, facing Blake's door. I wanted to see him coming, to face him head on. And because I wanted that, I must have sensed Emma's need for protection, although it could never be said that her behavior lent a clue to her need.

Decades have passed, but some things I still miss. Not very many. Certainly not Blake, although I can't seem to erase the memory of him. Emma. Certainly Emma, when I get past a personal sense of betrayal and remind myself that it wasn't a socially conditioned covetousness that drew me to her. It was, quite simply, just Emma.

Whatever her external form, the remarkable qualities would have shone through. Openness, vibrancy, resilience. She defied and resisted categorization. She was not female, white, brunette, or middle-class Protestant; she was not a Georgetown graduate, a Florida native, a holdover '60s idealist, or a Poverty Law Center attorney. My act of conceiving this list, its blackness on whiteness, mirrors our faces, and probably says more about me than about her. In my mind's eye she reacts—incredulous, without disdain.

Some other things I miss: pulling on a pair of khakis and a polo shirt, walking to the office in that perpetual Florida sunshine, eating a messy sandwich for lunch at the park across the street. Sometimes with Emma, sometimes the three of us. The camaraderie of a shared purpose, the downtrodden holding hands against the world. The excitement of youth, intelligence, and idealism—my belief in idealism, until it faded. Transformed is a better word, for the only thing I've discarded is Blake's type of altruism, his establishment idealism.

He would laugh to hear me say that. "*Establishment* idealism? Who's the real establishment figure here, Verne?" Today, so many years later, he would still call me Verne, although I never invited him to shorten my full name, Vernon.

Just like PLC days, I want to see what's coming. I've positioned my desk so that I face the door when seated. Every once in a while, I visualize Blake, frozen in my memory at age thirty-four, entering my office, this time knocking first. He steps in with his flaxen curls of the '70s and elbow-patch jacket, allowing his blue eyes to sweep the room before he speaks.

"Cushy. Pretty cushy," he says with a grin, afraid to articulate his true thoughts out of concern for political correctness. This is a gray zone for him. Am I a sell-out or a role model? What he really thinks, I see in his eyes: Look at you, so well scrubbed and benign in your hand-tailored suit, behind your mahogany desk. Litigating expensive cases for millionaires. Have you forgotten where you came from? Have forgotten who you are— your people?

I always have the perfect response: Yes, I'm an expensive lawyer, but I do my share of *pro bono* cases, working free for the poor. My practice is scrupulously ethical. But none of this really matters to you. There were things about me you never took the time to learn.

And I say: No, I haven't forgotten where I came from. We didn't have material things, but I had enough to eat, a stable home, a mother and father who loved each other, worked hard and cared. I suffered my share of nasty looks and closed doors but was spared my share of violence.

And I haven't forgotten who I am. Not merely a dark brown face within a smudged sea of bronze to black. I'm Vernon Thomas Sotherland Jr., husband of Ruby Lynn, father of Leora, Amity, and Reginald. These are my people, and the hundreds of others their lives will touch, a spectrum of color and individuality. How I treat them and what I teach them will spread and grow. Stability, respect, commitment, and love.

Of course, Blake always listens to me and nods his agreement. Something he never did back then.

Goosenecked over our transcripts, Emma and I would tilt up at the sound of the door, anticipating Blake's voice. "What's happening at Willie's trial?" he would ask day after day, as if we'd just returned from court. The defendant, Jones, had become "Willie," just as Emma was "Emmie," and I was "Verne." Lucky for me, Verne was an easy stopping place between Vernon and Vernie.

When he assigned the trial record, Blake disassembled it like a sandwich, two slices of bread for me, ham and cheese for Emma. My top slice was the beginning section, the part with the pretrial hearings and jury selection, and the bottom slice was the sentencing hearing at the end, after Jones had been convicted. Emma got the guts of the trial: the opening statements, the witnesses' testimony, the summations, and the court's instructions to the jury.

Slowly, I came to understand Blake's motivation for this division of labor. From Emma he wanted a legal technician, someone to spot the technical procedural issues that arise at trial. But from me, Blake was looking for something more, a social and political ally. My part of the transcript contained most of the juicy issues he thrived on. Were the cops just looking to hassle another black man when they searched the defendant's car? Were blacks selectively excluded from the jury in favor of closet racists? When the judge chose death, did he ignore Willie's disadvantaged background, his victimization, all those social forces that molded him, quite involuntarily, into a killer?

I looked for the answers to these questions, the answers I knew Blake wanted to hear, but day after day, I failed to find them. They just weren't there. William Douglas Jones, serial killer, was important to the police and prosecutors, and they'd been very, very careful every step of the way, building an airtight case and trying Jones on the one murder with the most compelling evidence.

Emma, too, wasn't giving Blake the answers he needed. "There's really nothing here," Emma told him one Friday morning when she'd nearly finished reading her portion of the trial. It was the day I began to see things. "This is the cleanest transcript I've ever read."

Blake smiled. "In your long career."

"In my very long and distinguished tenure with this

esteemed organization."

"Such as it is, Emmie."

"Yes."

Emma had turned in her chair to face Blake, and her profile was visible to me. She smiled wanly, her repartee falling flat. Blake took the four steps from his doorway to the space between Emma's desk and mine and stood behind her chair, peering down at the open transcript on her desk. All but a sliver of Emma disappeared from my view, behind Blake. He seemed to be standing very close to her, his beltline even with the top of Emma's head, and he touched her shoulder—that much I could see. Not so unusual for Blake, a person who touched frequently as proof of his warmth and connection to humankind.

"What am I going to do with you two?" asked Blake, his back to me, massaging Emma's shoulder. He lifted his hand, pointed a finger at Emma's head, and buzzed an imitation of a ray gun. "The thought police have sucked out your brains! You've metamorphosed into fledgling Assistant County Attorneys! Give me that transcript! Just give it to me!" He leaned over her head and lifted the huge binder of onion skin a few inches from the desk, then let it fall, as if it were too heavy for him.

All of this was a joke of course. There was a lot of joking. Blake had a way about him, and I could sense Emma's smile without seeing her face. He hooked a strand of her waist-length dark hair and stroked it between finger and thumb. This seemed too intimate, even for Blake, but Emma didn't react.

"There is one thing," she said.

"Oh, she's found *one* thing. The trial is almost over

and there's *one* thing!" Blake looked backward over his shoulder, not at me exactly, but as if to remember me, and he replaced Emma's strand of hair.

"A little rhetorical flourish by the prosecutor during the summation."

"A flourish," Blake said with a French accent.

"Here's what the prosecutor said." She started to read: "'Just imagine it, ladies and gentlemen. Mary Griffin coming home from work, just two blocks to go, almost home, and this defendant waiting in the shadows, a snake in the grass, viper's fangs dripping, coiled up for the strike.'"

"Animalistic metaphors. Reversible error. New trial." Blake whirled around to gauge my reaction, looking for a sting on personal sensibilities. Emma's big find bordered on my area of "expertise"—the thing that Blake needed me for—and he was testing me.

Unimpressed, I said nothing, just shrugged my shoulders. I doubted that the jurors had convicted Jones out of a mistaken belief that he was a poisonous snake in need of extermination.

Blake wouldn't take a shrug for an answer. He needed dialogue, and his blue eyes bore into me, looking for a response. "Maybe snakes don't offend you? What if the prosecutor called Willie a chimp or gorilla? One of those nasty ape metaphors?"

The blood rose to my face, a reaction invisible to Blake's eyes, which only saw the surface. There was nothing I could hope to say that wouldn't be sapped of credibility in the heat of Blake's intensity and conviction.

"That's the trouble, Verne," he went on. "You need

to put yourself in Willie's shoes, sit at the defense table next to your sweaty, inept, underpaid court-appointed attorney and see how it feels to be called a dripping-fanged viper, knowing you're innocent of this heinous crime."

"Innocent?" I managed.

"You, Verne. We're talking about you. Did *you* kill Mary Griffin? The cops are circling the ghetto one night and they spot you in your rusty Cadillac and say, 'well, he fits the description.' Five-ten, one-sixty, dark-skinned Negro. It's all so scientific, Verne. You know you're innocent. You know you're the type of guy who brakes for squirrels. But it doesn't matter to them. The cops know they're right, and even if they're wrong, to them you look like the kind who could rape and mutilate their white daughters and sisters, so they search your car, maybe plant a few of Mary's hairs from the crime scene. They give you this sorry mistake of a defense lawyer, put you on trial for murder, and to top it off, they call you a venomous reptile, coiled for the strike. How does it feel now, Verne? How does it feel?"

I couldn't speak, and I hated myself for it, as much as I hated Blake in that moment. I kept my eyes on him, knowing that I needed to show this small kernel of strength while I grappled with the decency (or timidity) that prevented me from expressing my rage at his insult and his obliviousness to it. I groped for Emma with invisible touch and sensed the quality of her energy. There was a change in her. The awe and delight she often expressed for Blake's little expositions had been replaced with a tired sort of annoyance.

"I, I have trouble with that," I said finally.

"Trouble with what?"

"With the concept of the defendant's—*this* defendant's, innocence." I caught myself before the nickname "Willie" slipped from my mouth, sure that Blake's habit of using diminutives was just as objectionable when applied to a serial killer.

Blake took a single step toward his door, swiveled to face me once again, and laughed like a father would laugh at an erring child, sure of his superior knowledge and experience, but good-natured, without malice. "Then why are you here? Why are you helping this son of a bitch?"

Feeling the hot seat, I couldn't prevent a glance at Emma, hoping my desperation didn't show. In that glance we shared the knowledge of Blake's ploy. He couldn't possibly believe in Jones's innocence, although he never would admit it.

"The death penalty is unfairly applied to some and not others," I said. "Besides, the Constitution guarantees a fair trial for everyone. We're defending all our rights here, not just this defendant's."

In Blake's smile I saw recognition of his philosophy—the part I still believed and had successfully mimicked—before his face changed to that look of inviolable sincerity, a familiar, convincing expression. "A nice thing, Verne. A nice side benefit. But your client isn't the Constitution. Your client is Willie Jones. And how can you be so sure of his guilt? Who's God here? How do you know that, ten years after Willie fries in the chair, you won't hear about the new evidence that proves this was all a big mistake?"

Leaden silence hung between us, and then, instantly, I was invisible again. Blake had turned his eyes on Emma, and he stared hard at her for seconds that ticked with inevitability. She was frozen in her chair, boldly returning his stare while he stood above us with arms crossed, evaluating the extent of her resistance.

"Life," he said like a preacher, his voice scratchy with emotion. He paused before continuing, still looking at Emma. "Life is here and gone in an instant. Think about it, Verne." An invisible Verne.

Blake didn't want my answer and he didn't wait for Emma's but turned to go. At his office door, before closing it behind him, he remembered me and aimed the ray gun. "Find something," he said.

Emma turned away from Blake's door and sat with her back to me, hunched over her transcript. Stillness. For a long time, I waited to hear the crackle of turning pages.

Later that day, Emma did another new thing. She recruited me as her ally in a lunchtime escape from the office. I'd had lunch with Emma many times, but never in a sneaky way, always very open. Informally, but in compliance with an unspoken rule, we would tell Blake we were stepping out, giving him the opportunity to join us or not, as he pleased. A yell through the door was enough.

An hour or so after Blake's retreat, while his door was still closed, Emma turned to me and whispered, "I have to get out of here. Come on."

The command confused then overwhelmed me in the moment it took to understand its significance.

Without hesitation, I stood to join her. Neither of us yelled at Blake through the door.

Outside, the immense sunshine and diffuse heat were a relief from our sweltering box. On the way to the park she said, "Do we need to stop at the deli? I'm not very hungry, are you?"

"No," I lied.

"Look, there's some shade."

We were lucky enough to find a bench under the mimosa tree, and she offered an apple she'd been carrying in her handbag. I accepted it gratefully, uttering a few words that diminished my need for it. The important thing was to be alone with her, to be favored with her request for my exclusive company, out from under the imminent presence of Blake.

"I didn't know you had a rusty Cadillac."

"Neither did I." Our eyes met, and we both smiled before she looked away, gazing into the distance.

A moment later, "He can be a bit much sometimes, can't he?" She turned to me again, this time her eyes wide with sadness. So beautiful in her sadness.

"More than a bit," I said.

"I used to find that attractive. I saw only the good intentions, and his belief in his good intentions. But he's blind to a few things about himself, isn't he?" She didn't expect me to answer. Her mouth turned up into a little smile that told me she could imagine being inside darker skin and could feel what it was like being me, listening to Blake, but would never presume her entitlement to frame that feeling in words and demand my agreement. I thanked her silently for that and knew then that I loved her.

The moment was soon gone. "I won't be at work on Monday," she said. "Maybe Tuesday too, depending. I know it's a bad time to take off, but there's something I've got to do. I can't get out of it. Sorry to leave you alone with Blake."

"I'll survive. But what's—"

"How's Nadine doing?"

"Nadine," I echoed. My girlfriend at the time, a law student, a woman I liked very much but did not love. Early on, when I'd begun to doubt that I had a chance with Emma—or that I should risk the consequences even if she had some interest—I may have verbally puffed Nadine's significance, just to let Emma know I wasn't a sorry fellow. "She's doing just fine," I said.

"This is her last year?"

"Yes. Studying hard already. Toward finals, she'll vanish completely." Not such a sorry fellow, but maybe left alone at times. That was the implication, something for Emma to pick up on, if she wished.

Emma smiled again, still low. "You're a lucky man."

"Lucky?"

"To have a big love. Some of us just have mistakes. Mistakes that breed other mistakes."

At that moment I didn't understand. Not many days later, I would discover Emma's "mistake" in my memory of the countless little things I'd failed to evaluate. But for then, my discovery not yet made, her mistake took the form of a ponderous, nameless thing, a tragedy for her, and the messenger of my failed opportunity.

Inside, I cried out to her. *Emma, my big love.* She leaned toward me and put her head on my shoulder, and we sat that way in silence for a long time, people walking by, wondering.

That Monday, Emma gone, Blake proposed we do our field work, and we set off early for the penitentiary. This would be my first visit with a convicted murderer. Keith had always been the one to accompany Blake on these interviews with our clients, but now it was my turn.

The car trip took a good two hours. I'd spent a lot of time with Blake but never such a long time alone with him, no one and nothing else to distract us. No possibility of escape.

Early into the trip, its dual purpose became apparent to me. Blake's anger sought an outlet, and I became his target, the recipient of biting remarks and petty sarcasm that soon developed into bigger issues. Confused more than threatened, I did little to defend myself. I'd done nothing to deserve his ire, except, perhaps, to be the unfortunate, daily reminder to him of something beyond our control: we hadn't a prayer of helping Jones.

We'd found no surprise evidence of his innocence, no illegal police conduct, no unfair trial tactics. There were a few small complaints about the proceedings—the "viper" comment one of them—enough to fill an appellate brief, but nothing momentous enough to require reversal of his conviction. Still, we maintained a small hope of winning a reduction in his sentence from death to life imprisonment, and for that, we were looking for mitigating circumstances, anything from Jones's background or personality to arouse the court's sympathy and speak for clemency.

Blake, of course, sensed that I wasn't as passionately committed as he to saving Jones from the electric chair. In the course of reading the proof against Jones, I'd developed a visceral hatred of the man, an emotion that didn't easily lie low. An eye for an eye was not a difficult concept for me where William Douglas Jones was concerned, and by the time we neared the end of our trip to the pen, I came to believe that this was the source of Blake's anger: his frustration at being unable to mold my views to his own.

"You ever fried a living snake, Verne?"

From the passenger side of the front seat I glanced at Blake, hoping that his casual manner of steering the car—right wrist atop the steering wheel, left elbow out the open window—was a disguise for innate attentiveness and dexterity. "No," I said.

"Probably not something you'd enjoy watching."

"Doubt it."

"I never fried one either, but I bet it would jump and squirm and pop for a long time before it died. A long time." He let that one rest for a couple of miles before he continued. "It's easy to sit in the office and smell Emmie's perfume and read a transcript. Easy at a distance to pass judgment and let someone else do the killing. But today you're going to see the flesh on Willie's bones. Flesh just like your own." He momentarily took his eyes off the road and flicked them at my face and hair, recording my features for easy reference and comparison later on. "When you see Willie, think of that flesh jumping and sizzling."

"Blake, you know I've been working on this case.

Working hard on it."

"Blacks who kill whites get death five times more than whites who kill blacks. Think about it when you're talking to Willie."

"Don't you think I know that? Don't you think that's why I'm here?"

"But I know damn well you won't lose a night of sleep if Willie fries! You or Emmie."

"You can't say that about Emma."

He turned and looked at me longer than safety allowed. Icy blue. "Our hypocritical little Emmie, out taking care of business today!" He laughed and turned his eyes back on the road. "So she really wants to save Willie, but other little people aren't worth the bother? Maybe there's some distinction here I'm not getting. Maybe you know more about the way she thinks than I do. All that time together in your office, all those lunches in the park. So what did she tell you? She's done her own study on the condemned, his identity, his traits, and his lineage. Who is he, Verne? Where did he come from? Who's responsible for him? We know the mother, but do we ever know the father? Sometimes the color of his face can't hide his identity and society scorns him, so why not make it easier? Let's execute him and prevent another life of pain. Isn't that what Emmie really thinks? *Isn't it?*"

The emotion showed, and he was aware of it. He held back then, and we didn't speak again until we reached our destination, while I silently evaluated my memories—the looks, the touches, the times they'd been together alone. My heart sank low.

* * *

The prison was just as I'd imagined it. Two guards led us down an echoing linoleum corridor, the air stale with antiseptic and body odor. Death row might have been worse than death, something easier to lose sleep over than the finality of the electric chair.

But when I saw Jones, there wasn't much about his flesh to arouse my sympathy. Never having laid eyes on us before, he had difficulty understanding that we were there to help him. Physically and verbally he expressed his distrust. Before letting us near him, the guards made much of shackling Jones by his wrists and ankles to a chair bolted into the floor.

"We're your lawyers, man," said Blake, over and over.

"Ain't no lawyers," spat Jones, looking at me alone. He was missing half his teeth, and the remaining ones were large and yellow. I thought of the medical examiner's testimony: the bite marks in distinctive patterns.

Blake was louder than Jones and thoroughly convinced of his beliefs, giving him the ability to tranquilize the irrational with his own form of reasoned zealousness. Our client eventually understood and quieted enough to be interviewed. For the next half hour, we—mostly Blake—peppered him with questions, hoping to learn something encouraging that couldn't be gleaned from the court papers and written psychiatric reviews in our possession.

The chains rattled, shoes scuffed linoleum, and desperate laughter burst from Jones's lips between his two favorite sentences: "I'm innocent," and "Ask Mama." Blake failed to chip anything else loose, and we eventually surrendered to the prisoner's recalcitrance. Not having much else to go on, we decided to take Jones's advice and visit his mother, who lived a short distance from the penitentiary.

We didn't speak during the next leg of our journey, or later, on our way back to the office. Knowing what we suspected about one another, we couldn't possibly talk about the case or pretend an interest in our work. Under the hum of engine and traffic noise, I thought of a time, a year ago, when I was so taken with Blake I would have asked every naïve question about what he thought and knew, his psychological profile of our client and how it might help us in our fight for his life.

Briefly, I longed for that time, but my thoughts kept returning to Emma and the hideousness of Blake's confusion of thought, his mixture of victims, condemned murderers, and executioners, the lines smudged, individual colors and circumstances indistinguishable through the narrow reference of his jealousy and personal need, the emotions and biases facilely disguised as political platforms.

But my judgment of Blake caught up with me the moment we arrived in "Mama's" neighborhood, a row of houses not unlike the block I grew up on, very poor but neat. I was surprised that Jones had grown up in a house like mine, and I was reminded how easy it was to fall into the comfort of categories. Blake was guilty of this need for comfort, but weren't we all? And maybe Blake felt more keenly about others and distinguished more exactly than I gave him credit. He loved Emma, that much was clear. Loved her so deeply he was sick over it.

We knocked at the front door and were allowed entry. Jones's mother was a wisp of a woman, apparently stick thin under her shapeless cotton dress. Three or four adolescents wandered in and out of the living room as we talked, Blake and I on a lumpy couch, Mrs. Jones in a rocking recliner. The room was sparse, the surfaces rubbed to inner layers with age. A thick green glass ashtray sat on the low coffee table in front of us, a brass Jesus sagged on a cross affixed to the wall.

She offered us nothing and glanced upon us infrequently. Her eyes were vacant, devoid even of indifference. Trying to warm things up, Blake made small talk. "How many brothers and sisters does Willie have?"

"How many it say there?" She glanced at the folder in Blake's hand.

Caught in his knowing omission, Blake laughed and said, "Was it eight?"

"Could be it."

He went on to other subjects, asking how Willie had done in school as a child, what his interests were. Each time, her answer was about "them," her children, apparently one and the same. "They always be doin" this, or "they always talkin like" that. She seemed unaware of her son's murder conviction and incarceration, although Blake and I knew the opposite; she had been interviewed more than once by probation authorities who must have told her, even if she'd been oblivious to the extensive news coverage at the time of Jones's arrest and trial.

Perhaps hoping to provoke a response, Blake hinted at a few details of Willie's crimes, the torture and mutilation. "Allegations," Blake still called the facts. It was then that her expression changed for the first time, a slight turning of the mouth that, for her, could be called a smile.

"Finga'n'toe," she said. "They used to call it."

Blake probed until she explained.

"Pigs feet. I make a stew and that what they always call it: 'finga'n'toe pot.'"

Emma only needed the Monday off. She was back on Tuesday, looking pale and tired. We arrived before Blake, and when he came in, he said "good morning" and barked our assignments as he walked through our office on the way to his own, then closed the door behind him.

After some time, alarmed at Emma's pallor, I asked how she was, thinking I hadn't revealed anything in the way I asked. But she gave me a searching look, leaned forward in her chair, and whispered, "Blake told you, didn't he?"

Her eyes made it impossible for me to hide, and so I told the truth. "Yes, but not in so many words." Should I go the next step? "He also—" I couldn't finish the sentence, but it was too late.

"What Vernon? He also what?"

"He also... He suspects me as the father. *Me.*"

Her eyes widened. I couldn't stand to see her shock, and I glanced at Blake's closed door. "What did you say?" she whispered.

I kept my voice low. "Nothing. I didn't get it at first. He was talking about our lunches in the park—he must have seen us on Friday—and about Jones's mother and father and executions and...and then I got it."

She turned away from me, put her elbows on the desk, and buried her head in her hands. "I don't think I can see this case through, Vernon. I have to leave."

At that moment, Blake stepped in with an accusing look as if he'd heard us, although I knew he couldn't have. "You finished, Verne?"

"Not yet," I said, only two sentences on the yellow pad in front of me.

He looked at Emma. "Maybe you want to help Verne write up the summary of the mitigating circumstances. I'm sure you have some good ideas. Maybe this was a justified murder. Have we probed that angle yet? Did Mary Griffin deserve to die? Maybe Willie did us all a favor when he killed her. Or maybe he just *thought* she was someone who deserved to die. A case of mistaken identity. But that's okay, as long as he believed the world would be a better place without her. Right, Emmie? Some people shouldn't even be born, so why should Willie be electrocuted for that?"

"Stop it, Blake," said Emma.

"How about the psychological profile of a serial killer? All those women, one after another, it didn't much matter to him *who* he killed. Nothing personal against Mary Griffin, so what's so terrible about that? He was indiscriminate, unbiased. He picked up whoever was convenient, had a good time, tossed her away and picked up the next one. Not such offensive behavior, no bad feelings, no real malice involved—no love either—but so what? I could tell you about some people. Should we send someone to the chair for that?"

"Stop this! There wasn't anyone else! You're way

off—" Emma's lips trembled.

"We know someone like that, don't we, Verne?"

I jumped from my seat. Blake stepped backward, his eyes popping open with alarm, then narrowing defensively. He knew he'd gone too far.

"I've been thinking about this hard," I said.

"Oh?" His sarcasm sounded like a parody of himself.

"I have a mitigating circumstance. A new one, not one of those you mentioned. It's one you haven't considered."

Blake and Emma kept their silence, as if they were relieved, my interruption saving them from each other.

"It came to me when we visited Mrs. Jones and I saw the way she regarded her own son, no more than one of her nine children, just another head in a swarm of heads. If there'd been anything unique about him when he was growing up, any small talent or interesting trait or special feature, she didn't notice or acknowledge it. His individuality was wasted and became emptiness. And whatever the reason, maybe it was a predisposition, Jones filled that emptiness with every bad impulse and desire. He wasn't seen, and he's angry. He may not know it, but he wanted to be seen, because that's what each one of us really wants. We want to be seen and heard apart from everyone else."

Emma stood then, and we were all standing, our eyes darting from one to the other, shame and pride dividing us. Emma picked up her handbag, I picked up my briefcase, and we walked out the door.

My final words to Blake may have been my finest, but I

felt no righteousness or glory in them. For once, I had spoken my mind, but it was a small piece of a much larger map leading to so many thoughts and ideas left unsaid.

He had the decency, at least, to avoid retribution. He could have punished us for leaving him high and dry, alone with Willie, but he gave us only the most glowing recommendations when future employers called to inquire about our performance at PLC. And from what I heard, within a few weeks, he was fortunate enough to hire two decent attorneys to replace his wayward fledglings.

Emma and I kept in touch for a short time. She moved to D.C., joined a law firm, and soon after that stopped writing or calling. I moved to New York where I restarted my career, found my true "big love," and had a family.

And Blake, despite what I'm sure was a wholehearted effort, was unable to save William Douglas Jones. From afar, I kept abreast of the case, following it through a series of appeals and habeas corpus petitions until, ten years after I left PLC, Jones sat in the chair.

Just as Blake predicted, I didn't lose any sleep the night I learned of the execution, but I'd lost so much sleep during my PLC days and in the years since that I've never become a proponent of the death penalty. I maintain a tenacious belief in the statistical and ethical objections to government execution, arguments that are easy to conceive and embrace when sitting in an office, reading transcripts, remembering the smell of Emma's perfume.

∼QUICKER FORMS OF DEATH

HEATHER IS LOOKING dangerously sexy and unaware, as though everything Marie told her before coming here is blown straight out of her blonde head. Her hips are undulating in that shimmering minidress, pulsating in the strobe and samba beat. They're immersed in amplified Brazilian Portuguese, the lyrics swishing over the foreign vocalist's tongue, oozing all around.

Marie examines Heather's partner while pretending to dance with her own. He looks respectable enough in a designer sport jacket, his face well scrubbed with a manicured mustache—not the pencil-thin one of a pervert. Something Latin about him. Marie has noticed that Heather's California blondness jumps out in New York, and now it's especially apparent in this establishment, housing a combination of races, some with light hair but most with brown or black.

Heather is throwing her platinum tresses here and there with abandon, dancing close to this stranger she met just fifteen minutes ago, if you can call that a meeting—the exchange of glances, mouthed "hellos" under the deafening sound, lamb silently following wolf into the pack. But it's a public place and she will be all right, as long as Marie stays close and keeps an eye on her.

Marie begins to pay more attention to her own partner, thinking that, in this way, she might intuit something more about his friend, Heather's partner. She's fairly sure his name is Tony and he's a customer service rep at some bank—bits of information he shouted into her ear along with the spray of a warm mist from his mouth. She reciprocated, leaning toward his ear but careful not to touch, yelling her name and occupation as a paralegal, studying law at Columbia. He didn't flinch at her ambitions, a sign of either his strong character or her weak voice failing to pierce the din. Tony is six inches taller than Marie in her heels and has light olive skin and wavy brown hair. He moves naturally to the beat and appears introspective, as though inspired by the music.

Tony and Heather's partner approached them at the same time and in the same way, eyeing them first from across the room, sharing manly smiles and winks before winding and bumping through the crowd on a magnetic track. Marie saw them coming and let it happen while Heather shouted a few words of girlish anticipation into her ear. This was the purpose of their night out, fun and excitement, something Marie hasn't dared or even had time for recently with her nose always buried in books. The men in her classes haven't been much of a distraction. Marie started law school years after finishing college, and her classmates seem very young.

Summer vacation and Heather's visit, fresh from a breakup with her husband, made this night inevitable.

Marie's temporary freedom from school gives her an abundance of spare energy. Heather is also free of a burden—a four-year mistake—leaving her the gay divorcée at twenty-nine and ready for the fun she thinks she's been missing. "I feel like we're in high school again!" she said after their first all-night gabfest the day of her arrival. "Can you imagine, Marie, if I'd had a baby by that creep? Thank God I never got pregnant."

There's time for all that later, they agreed then, eyeing each other with looks that betray the fears of many women on the eve of thirty.

This night, Heather's second in the big city, they are *not* in the market for prospective husbands. Of course, anything is possible but highly unlikely at a bar like this, even if it *is* very popular and attracts perfectly normal people like Marie and Heather. Neither are they in the market for trouble, Marie reminded Heather before coming, and they have to keep an eye out for each other. They will stick together and leave together, no exceptions. Marie does not want to be tripping over strange men in her apartment the next morning. "Please, don't give anyone my address! Give them your number and address in California if you want, but not mine!" Marie felt the need to stress these points, what with Heather acting so carefree since the day she arrived, oblivious of every stranger that pressed up against her in the subway and on the street.

"Yes, mother," said Heather. "You know, he didn't keep me locked up in the house with the vacuum and I wasn't born yesterday."

"No, you don't understand," said Marie. "There's

only one real city in the world, New York City. Everywhere else is nowhere."

"Santa Barbara is nowhere? You know better, Marie. You weren't exactly the country hick when you came here. Even at St. Mary's we learned a few things!"

They laughed then, thinking of the nights they experimented with alcohol and boys.

Now, as she glances again at Heather, Marie resolves not to get drunk, not while she has her friend to look after. But she is out of practice with alcohol and is already feeling the effects of just one rummy piña colada. The rhythm is intoxicating too, a dozen unfamiliar percussion instruments driving deep into her core, sending her own hips in circles, not quite as freely as Heather's, but less inhibited than she would have imagined before coming here.

Tony catches her eye and she smiles timidly. "Having fun?" he yells, and she understands the words more from the shape of them on his mouth. "Yes," she nods. He keeps looking at her, forgetting his own internal rhythm, and his eyes shine with real interest. He's handsome, she decides, wondering how her own bookish look attracted such a man, then remembers what she's wearing: a scoop-necked, crimson dress that Heather pulled from a dormant spot in Marie's closet. "This is it!" exclaimed Heather, who busied herself with Marie's "look," pulling her thick mahogany hair up, off her slender neck, sticking it haphazardly with pins and allowing a few strategic wisps to stray into her face. With red lipstick—another forgotten article in her medicine cabinet—Marie is colorful and exotic.

Tony moves closer. After midnight the crowd starts to thicken, but Heather and partner are still within sight. They've been dancing for half an hour, but Marie isn't tired. The swish and juicy pulp of the Brazilian tongue infuses her movement with the deepest mystery, resplendent and infinite life pressing in on all sides, bodies swaying together like tall marsh reeds in the wind.

She doesn't stop Tony as he lifts her hands to his shoulders where she rests them lightly, trying not to feel the smooth muscle like a lion's back under his shirt. Tony takes her waist, and they bend their heads down to examine their hips, moving them in sync, rolling and bumping. Marie looks up, catches his eye and they laugh at their game.

The music and flashing lights stop; the band takes a break. Canned music comes over the speakers at a lower volume, and they break apart, standing awkwardly and stunned with the possibility of speech. They laugh nervously and exchange small talk: yes, Tony has come to this club before, but it's Marie's first time; he likes to go clubbing when he can, but she doesn't have much time, not with school and work.

Only when Heather stands a foot away is Marie startled into remembering that she hasn't seen her friend for a good five minutes. Heather's eyes aren't shy like Marie's; they shine with excitement as she holds her partner's hand. Heather leans toward Marie's ear: "I have to go to the bathroom!" To their partners they say, "Will you excuse us?" The men exchange looks before demanding, "You better come back, now!"

Tony and friend follow them to the ladies' room and

loiter outside while Marie and Heather go in. Heather, unable to wait, cuts in line. Marie holds the latch-less stall door for her and wonders if the men will be gone when they come out. But Heather has no intention of escape.

"What do you think of him?" she asks Marie through the closed door. "Isn't he good looking? He's so sweet too! How did we get so lucky right off?"

"He looks all right, but…"

Heather flushes the toilet and comes out, squirming, tugging her hem down. They go to the mirror. "This place is *so* much fun, Marie! You were right—there's nothing like it back home!"

Marie eyes her own hair, still magically arranged in the contrived, haphazard bun. "He looks all right, just, you know—"

Heather stops fussing over her hair and makeup and turns to Marie. "Here comes the lecture again."

"No, it's just…"

"And what's wrong with a little fling? I'm here for a week. I never have to see him again. Nothing but sweet memories."

"Or bad memories, or much worse. Diseases and quicker forms of death."

"Oh, I know all that. I know how to take care of myself! Let's just have some fun. Come on!"

The men are waiting exactly where they left them, now holding piña coladas for the women, straight shots for themselves. Tony and friend—Marie suddenly realizes she hasn't found out his name—are making jokes about women and their attachment to bathrooms as they offer the drinks. In a shockingly natural motion, Heather's free hand grasps her new friend's biceps as she leans up against him to talk.

Marie tries to keep her distance from Tony, but people are jammed in, squeezing around them, jostling her in a way that makes touching inevitable. Her eyes rest on Heather, then flit around the room, including Tony for split seconds, noticing his eyes unwaveringly on her with a gregarious charm—not threatening—a quality that undoubtedly adds to his success as a customer service rep at some bank.

Their chatter continues, the drinks are sipped and then gone, and the room is warm and fleshy and dreamlike, Marie's head filled with the buzz of laughter and conversation and recorded salsa or cha-cha or lambada or samba and Tony's regular, gleaming teeth in that charming smile. She looks at him for longer moments until her discomfort disappears and he seems like her oldest friend, the person she has trusted all her life.

At 1:15 the band is back on and talk is futile, so the happy four squish their way back onto the dance floor, joining the rising tide of rippling bodies. Heather and Marie are side by side, their male friends facing them, a nose length away. Heather throws her arms around her partner and his hands circle her waist, their hips swirling in a single motion like a wooden spoon stirring thick cake batter. Marie feels their hips bump hers on each revolution and now she thinks nothing of it, this natural, rhythmic motion, here in a public place where everyone can see and feel the same things without fear of consequence.

A rush of liberating feeling swells within, sending her closer to her own partner, letting him take her completely in a full-bodied embrace. He begins to pick the pins out of her hair, letting them fall to the ground one by one, her hair slowly coming undone on her damp neck. People on all sides are pressing in, their hips rubbing hers from behind and on both sides, his in front. Her head circles and falls backward as she enjoys the weight of her loose hair falling down to the middle of her back.

She feels her existence only, her heart beating, sending blood through her loose limbs. Time and thought have vanished. Her head is thrown back, opening the long curve of her neck. Something wet and warm presses into a spot where her bare neck meets shoulder.

Marie snaps upright and rigid, forcing an invisible barrier between his lips and her neck. The swollen crowd swims around her and she clutches her dizzy head, eyes darting, body turning right and left and in circles.

Heather is gone. Marie has allowed her to drift out to sea.

"Where's Heather?" she shouts at Tony. He responds with a puzzled expression, a shrug of his shoulders. "WHERE'S HEATHER?" she screams at the top of her lungs, her voice still muffled under the raucous vibration, not enough to cause a head to turn. But Tony apparently hears, and he shouts something back: "Didn't you…?" She shakes her head and moves closer, determined to hear, but he doesn't repeat himself and says only, "Come on." He grips Marie's hand firmly and leads her off the dance floor while she scans every face, searching frantically. Heather's blonde head, so unmistakable hours before, has been gulped and sent into the belly of undulant flesh.

Tony leads her out to the lobby where the amplified music is strangely distant. "Didn't you see them?" he asks, and she can hear distinctly now, as though they've surfaced from an underwater cavern. "I thought you saw what happened," he adds.

Marie stands in stunned silence.

"They were dancing next to us and he leaned over and told me they were leaving."

"Leaving?"

"Yeah, they're going somewhere, or he's taking her home, whatever. I thought she told you."

Heather leaving with a strange man? Marie feels sick, on the verge of tears. She expected something like this, but still the shock of it hits her hard. What are warnings for, except to go unheeded? *I wasn't born yesterday*, says Heather in Marie's head. *I know how to take care of myself!* Defensive words with the ring of adolescent inexperience.

"Are you sure?" she asks Tony. "Maybe they haven't left yet. Can we just go look?" She feels the need for his permission and he grants it with a fatherly nod of his head.

Marie takes his hand and leads this time, wedging between couples, singles, and groups. They cover the entire place, but the search is hopeless, the crowd too thick. She imagines a PA system like the one at the zoo. The music will stop and a hush will descend over a thousand heads: *"Heather Langley, meet your mother in the lobby. Heather Langley."* Marie suddenly feels foolish.

They return to the lobby. "You look really worried

about this," says Tony, his brow furled with concern. "Why don't I just take you home? She knows how to get to your apartment, right?"

"Thanks, but I'll just take a cab."

"You shouldn't stand out there waiting for a cab. They don't come around this neighborhood too often. I waited an hour one night."

"Oh, I don't think—"

"Believe me! Let me drive you, it's quicker." He smiles, and she feels that ease about him, the closeness she felt earlier. Certainly he's a nice person, a concerned person, and she would rather not take a cab alone at this hour. Once, late at night, she was frightened by a taxi driver of questionable sanity who spiced his incessant rattle with obscenities.

Still, she hesitates. Respectful of her reluctance, Tony suggests that she wait outside in the bright lights of the club while he gets his car, a few blocks away. "If you see a cab before I get back, go ahead. Maybe we'll meet some day in paradise!" He throws his hands up in smitten surrender and she laughs. A nice guy really.

And true to his prediction, she sees no taxis before he returns, seven minutes later. In a daze, sticky in the soupy July air, she's been watching the cars go by as she imagines the one that Heather might have gotten into with her nameless companion. It's a bit like the one that Tony pulls up in, a black Trans Am with a souped-up engine and a blaring radio—not surprising since Tony, after all, is a friend of Heather's partner. Marie accepts it without judgment while her mind whirls with involuntary images: Heather with that man in a deserted building or by the waterfront or in a dark alley.

"Still here?" he says with laughing eyes, coming around to open the door for her like a gentleman. She smiles and gets in. The car is dark inside as well as out, Latin music throbbing. "Sorry," he says, slipping behind the wheel. He turns the volume knob. "I feel lonely without this on—when I'm alone that is."

He takes off aggressively into the traffic and Marie is suddenly annoyed at the male urge to impress a woman with speed. But she can't hold it against him, not after the sensitivity he's shown in other ways. She tells him her street and the cross streets so he'll know where to go, and says, "I appreciate this—you being so understanding."

He glances at her and smiles broadly. "Glad to be of service."

Traffic is light but not sparse, filled with Sunday morning night clubbers. He drives fast up the avenue, changing lanes, weaving around anyone in his way on a race to make every green light. He's gone twenty blocks before she knows it, and soon she'll be home.

Marie shakes her head. "I still can't believe it, Heather going off like that. We had an agreement. I hope she's there... Oh my God!"

He shoots her a look with raised eyebrows like, *what is it now?*

"I didn't give her the keys! She can't get in!" Tony hits the brakes; he has lost the race with a light. Only four blocks left to go. She looks at him pleadingly. "Did your friend say anything to you, I mean anything about where they were going?"

He returns her gaze with a sleepy-lidded, blasé look.

"What friend?" His eyes slip down to her hemline then back up her body, resting at the edge of her scooped neckline. He slides his hand along the slippery leather seat until it touches her thigh.

"Your friend! The guy with Heather! What's his name anyway?"

He doesn't seem to hear. Lifting his hand, he traces her neckline with a hot index finger. "Bud, or something like that," he says, his eyes glassy.

She squirms and moves away, but his hand is on the steering wheel again and he jerks forward into traffic a half second before the light turns green.

"What do you mean, 'something like that'?"

"Like what?"

"Like 'Bud, or something like that.' What's his name?"

"Bud, Bert, how the hell do I know? I just met the dude. How can you hear anything in that place?"

Tony is racing again, making every light—*so they aren't friends, not really*—three blocks, four, five and six. Her heart is pounding. She sees her mistake. "You—you missed my street, Tony. Please…"

He turns and stares at her too long before caring to notice the obstacles in the road ahead as he bullets through one light and the next. She wonders if the joke is true, that you can make the timed lights on the avenues in three ways—at 30, 60, or 90—and maybe Tony isn't doing 60, but there's no way she can jump out. "Relax," he says, "they're not at your apartment."

If she just keeps up a charade of normalcy, every-thing might be normal again. "Where?" she asks. "Where did he say…?"

Tony throws her another look, the drunken amusement gone from his eyes, replaced with a gleam of snide control. "He said *nothing* to me. Get it, Mother Teresa? *Nothing.* They're probably somewhere screwing their brains out right now. That friend of yours—she was hot for anything!" His hand slips over to finger her thigh again. "Relax and we'll have some fun."

Fifteen or more blocks past her street, every light is green—never green when you have to be somewhere, and she doesn't have to be where he's taking her. But his luck is running out as he hits the first yellow, zipping through three more yellows, each one getting closer to red. Finally, he screeches to a stop, his fingers hooked under the edge of her hemline. She opens the door and falls halfway out, but his fingers claw into the material and he leans over the seat to the door and yells, "Get in here!" His grasp is strong, but she summons the strength of fear and jerks away, leaving him to peer out the open passenger door with a jagged swatch of crimson material in his hand. She weaves in and out of the stopped cars, touching hoods, meeting curious eyes, not daring to look back.

When Marie gets to her apartment building, Heather is pushed into a corner of the well-lit vestibule, her face streaked with tears. Muggings, rapes, and even murders happen in vestibules, the criminal following his mark through the open, outer door, catching her off guard before she can get to the inner door and insert the key. Or before her friend gets home with the keys.

"Heather, are you all right? What did he do?"

"Nothing," says Heather with a glare that tells Marie she's the one who has caused the tears. "Why did you leave me there! I looked *everywhere* for you! We had an agreement!"

"Then you didn't… Oh, Heather, I looked for you too! Here, we have to get in." Marie opens the door, and safely inside the hallway, she dares once again to regard Heather's expression with its veiled accusation of betrayal. Marie bursts into tears. The women embrace and fall away, facing one another, shuddering and sobbing, not making a move to the elevator.

Marie speaks when she's able. "So, you didn't let him drive you home?"

"He didn't have a car. He was so sweet. He flagged a cab for me but didn't try to get in or even ask for my phone number. He gave me his number and said he would leave it all up to me."

"What was his name?"

"Butch."

"Butch?"

Heather smiles. "His students gave him that nickname. He's a high school teacher. I guess it couldn't be a Catholic school."

"I guess not." Marie smiles, then Heather giggles, and they both break out laughing.

"Maybe that wouldn't be so bad—the wife of a high school teacher in New York," says Heather through her laughter, but her face falls and suddenly she's half crying, half laughing. "What am I going to do? What?" A sob chokes her throat. "I'm twenty-nine and a salesclerk and you're a lawyer or practically a lawyer and one day I'm going to wake up and say, 'I'm forty-nine and I'm a sales-clerk.' What else *is* there? What am I going to *do*?"

Marie puts an arm around Heather and guides her toward the elevator, searching for words to express the admiration she feels for her friend's innate strengths—the qualities Marie lacks. But maybe the words will come later.

For now, she can't seem to shake those final moments, the shock of Tony's steely intensity and clutching grasp, her terror and mad dash. Her mind clouds with self-doubt, the lapse in perception and judgment, and all she can feel is the weight of her failure.

≋MALOCCLUSION

"THE ODDEST PART of it is…," the patient looked down at her hands in search of an elusive synapse, "I don't remember his name."

Dr. Reckner took full advantage of her downward gaze to roam the contours of her face, the border of carefully misplaced, highlighted strands of brunette, evidence of her attempt at youth. He lingered along the periphery for now, studiously avoiding the mouth, the universal center of need and desire: sustenance, communication, gratification.

A strange habit for someone in his profession, but his first inclination—more of a trained practice—was to look everywhere but the mouth, to gather in the person, beginning his study of the problem from the endpoint of its consequences, tracing those outer layers of symptomatic adjustment backward to their source, to the malocclusion. A soft tendril graced her temple and tipped at the point of a faint crow's foot. Another one caught in a lash near the delicate bridge of her nose, sending shudders up to the hairline with every blink.

To remind himself of her name, he glanced quickly at

the manila folder on his desk, its green-edged label color coded for the middle of the alphabet, L-M-N. Janine Lindstrom. Mrs. Lindstrom wasn't old, but neither was she young, and the haphazard bangs failed to conceal a three-quarter-inch crevice between her eyebrows, etched there, he knew, by her mouth. Everything came from the mouth.

He suspected that her age would come into stark relief once he escorted her away from the soothing, low wattage of his office into the adjoining room, where he would invite her to recline in the examination chair while directing the unforgiving high beam down into her core. He looked forward to that moment while enjoying these preliminaries, the easy foreplay to his ultimate, exacting handle on her problem.

"Try as I might, I can't remember!" Perhaps the doctor was God. She latched onto him with lost, pleading eyes. He quickly searched them, feeling the tug of a familiar cord—the first step toward his gradual descent. He also saw the pain in her eyes, had known he would find it there even before looking, but the beauty remained. What a waste! Years of waste, and all from the mouth. Still he avoided it, that shadowy maw lurking beneath the pretty nose.

"I was certainly old enough to remember something like that. A name. I was fourteen and fifteen. The treatment ended when I was sixteen. The whole experience was so painful I must have developed a mental block against it. The name that is." She issued a lusty sigh, surprising for its contrast to her bare murmur of a voice. "The rest of it I can't forget." Her head bobbed and fell to regard her wringing hands once more.

With the downward motion of her head, so went his, dropping below the neck, reaching forbidden territory, rebounding. He would have liked to remain there, exploring her unrealized corporal beauty—something he'd sensed (without looking) five minutes earlier when Mrs. Lindstrom had followed him into his office, heating his back with round suggestions under the puritan clothing. Her anxious gait was tense and bottled instead of free and easy the way nature would dictate if not for the influence of the mouth. That mouth.

At fourteen (before the damage had been done) the budding flower must have been irresistible. Dr. Reckner pushed the thought from his mind and averted his eyes, searching out the sterling-framed photograph on his desk, equidistant from doctor and patient, angled for the benefit of both. His wife Clarissa and their two teenagers, Bradford and Jake, displayed an abundance of dental glow, mouths he'd crafted to perfection.

"I remember my mother driving me there, and I have a vision of the street and the building and the waiting room—and the examining room. Recently, I went back to the place I thought it would be, but nothing looks the same. I have no other clues. Names in the phone book mean nothing to me. He would be quite old by now, and for all I know he's already dead. Believe me, I'd look him up if I could. I'd make him account for this! That man ruined my life!" Her eyes flashed at the doctor, and he swallowed hard on the wad of anxiety that always bubbled up at the suggestion of a lawsuit against one of his brethren.

A disgruntled neurotic, a person overly sensitive to pain and unrealistically convinced of entitlement, was a doctor's worst nightmare, could put the blight on career, reputation, and financial security. Mrs. Lindstrom seemed the type, but he hadn't yet completed his examination, and so, couldn't judge. Possibly her statements had real basis in fact. A mouth could ruin a life, he'd seen it before.

More from self-preservation than from a need to see the ancient x-rays of this woman's mouth, the doctor feigned interest: "Perhaps your family kept records," he suggested, "your parents—"

"Are dead."

"I'm sorry."

"Thank you, but they died many years ago. A horrible car accident. They were on their way to visit me at college."

"I'm so sorry."

"Yes, well, even then I was in some pain from this," she motioned to her mouth, "but didn't think to save my parents' old bills and records. After their death, my brother and I sifted through so much of their stuff. Why do we need to save this, we said? A bunch of old orthodontic records? I remember holding that file and looking at it, hesitating before I threw it in the trash. Who would have thought?"

"Yes, who would have?"

"I was in denial, you see. I'd been through treatment, I'd gone through all that pain and was supposed to have a perfect mouth as a result." Her small voice quavered. "And there I was, even then in college, only a few years after treatment, already with headaches, a pounding in my ears, clicking and jaw dislocation, lumps of food I couldn't chew, indigestion, and reflux."

"All from the mouth."

"Yes."

"The bite."

"Yes."

"And I'd venture to guess, it has gradually worsened over the years? The teeth, positioned badly, tend to shift."

"Yes!" She looked at her savior, the man who understood. "Yes, you know the problem exactly. My friend, the one who recommended you, said you were the only orthodontist to consult."

The doctor nodded modestly. He was, indeed, well regarded. Would go so far, in his own mind, as to say he was the best in the East Bay.

"I've waited a long time, I know."

The doctor nodded amiably.

"My dentist tells me, year after year, it's nearly impossible to correct, and it's risky to move my teeth. I may lose them. But I can't tolerate the pain any longer."

"No, and why should you?"

"Yes, why? But, Doctor—" She stopped on the edge of her words, a voice no more than a whisper and a gasp of air, pushing color into her cheeks. She hesitated, hovered, waiting for a response from him, waiting for a sign of irrepressible curiosity. All of it, a danger signal. Yes, why? What else could she be asking of him? He couldn't deny his need to know.

With a sage twist of the brow, he leveled his eyes on hers, fighting the growing urge to let them drop. "Yes, you'd like to know…?"

"Is it too late?"

His eyes went hard to the point of their intercourse. *Is it too late?* He saw her lips opening and closing in slow motion, words crawling through the tiny, withered, painted hole—*too*—a push and pucker—*late*—a pull and stretch. Her speech barely added shape to her mouth, what was visible of it on the surface, the greater part sunken deep inside her head without the support of teeth, a skinny dash with its sad attempt at enlargement: a thick layer of lipstick, a conservative mauve, extending above and below the lips into surrounding skin. It was the mouth of a gummy eighty-year-old, shrunken and lined, set within a rigid jaw marked with the unmistakable traces of clenching and gnashing, the flex of stressed muscles and tendons.

He straightened up against an involuntary shudder, successfully concealing it.

"Let's take a look at you," he said and stood, holding his hand out, motioning toward the open door into the examining room.

Dr. Reckner had seen many poorly aligned teeth, but none quite as bad as this. "Re-do's" and adult cases accounted for a large percentage of his practice, the middle-aged mothers and fathers of his preteen patients and their referrals, patients like Mrs. Lindstrom. Fairly immune to the sight of disfigured mouths, he'd shuddered not so much from the sight of hers as from the abominable thought of a doctor (someone who called himself a doctor, a member of his profession!) committing such a heinous act on the teeth of another human being.

From a long line of distinguished dentists, and as the second in his family to practice the specialty of ortho-dontics, David C. Reckner Jr., DDS, had maintained and built upon the legacy of David Sr. A solid reputation such as his wasn't seriously threatened by the butchers, hacks, and incompetents in his field, but still, his laurels moaned in outrage at any senseless deconstruction of a mouth.

Some consideration had to be taken, he knew, of the significant strides in the field of orthodontics since the days of Mrs. Lindstrom's first treatment. Even so, he couldn't pin her mouth on a competent dentist, one strapped by the ignorance of a science in its infancy. After all, hadn't his own father labored under the same state of incomplete knowledge—with excellent results?

Orthodontics was an art more than science, requiring that rare blend of muscular strength, precision, skill, vision, and sensitivity to gently prod the teeth into proper alignment, finding for the twenty-eight their ideal sixty-eight points of contact, a neat fit to the puzzle, all with an artist's intuitive eye on the natural contours of the mouth, cheeks, and jaw. A Michelangelo with hammer and chisel he was, chip-chip-chipping away at seemingly immovable, obtuse and resistant stone, rendering the ultimate aesthetic angle to a scrupulously smooth, mechanical, interlocking fit.

David Sr. had been a perfectionist, relieving thousands of malocclusions, and what better example than the mouth of his own son! David Jr. confirmed it every morning he awoke refreshed from a restful night of relaxed-jaw sleep, every time he bit into a carrot, every two years when he made yet another plaster impression of his own teeth (just to check!) and clacked the two beheaded jaws together in their perfect grooves. After all these years, each of the sixty-eight contact points remained perfectly aligned!

So, no, Mrs. Lindstrom's plight couldn't be blamed on an ancient age or a simpler time. A certain amount of common sense and humanity should have spared her from the butchery he found in her mouth. Pain was always involved—a criticism of his profession, that thoughtless question to which he was acutely sensitive: *Do you actually enjoy this infliction of pain?* But in her case, the pain must have exceeded the point of tolerance, for the best scenario he could fathom put her in the hands of a reckless dentistry school dropout—at worst, a downright sadist.

On the way to the examination chair, Dr. Reckner all but forgot that brief foreboding moment in his office. Mrs. Lindstrom was at once different. Relieved of her initial confession, she walked easier, allowing a show of life to the doctor, who followed closely enough to measure the greater breadth of his chest and shoulders on either side of hers while discretely consuming her backside from a pleasingly superior height. At the edge of the chair she lingered, touching it as if to remember, then hovered over it with her jutting, prudently covered tail, lowering herself familiarly into the curved joint of the seat before reclining fully, gently rotating the back of her head into the padded rest.

The doctor took his own stool, the round one on wheels. Moving in, sitting erect, he lowered Mrs.

Lindstrom's torso with the foot control while adjusting the overhead light, extending and fully exposing her prone form, chest rising and falling with every needful breath. Tension remained in the hush before each breath, in the clutch of her hands on the armrests. A large diamond in the wedding set on her left ring finger attested to another man's discovery of her finer qualities, a man who hadn't been fooled by that mouth.

"Marjorie," the doctor said, looking down into the orifice, absently holding the patient's manila folder out to the side. His assistant, arranging instruments in the corner, abandoned her task and turned toward him, hand outstretched for the folder. "Yes. Oh!" she said with a fleeting glance at the patient. Momentarily, her forward motion was arrested, and a tiny flush came into her apple cheeks before she took the folder and focused her full attention on it, pulling out the preprinted examination form with its black-on-white outlines of numbered teeth and lists of symptoms and diagnoses, all awaiting checkmarks and notations where appropriate.

Dr. Reckner didn't seem to notice the hesitation. Despite Marjorie's advancing years, she was quick and vital, an invaluable assistant. She put on her glasses and readied herself for the report, pulling a pen from jacket pocket.

With bare hands, warm, the doctor placed tips of index fingers, right and left, high into the symmetrical depressions of Mrs. Lindstrom's face, feeling for the hinges of her jaw, left and right. "Open and bite several times." She looked up at him and obeyed, deepening the crease between her eyes. Her skin went suddenly moist.

"TMJ locking," said the doctor. Marjorie dashed off a checkmark. He looked down into the patient's eyes, now flitting along the ceiling. "TMJ locking and pain," he said. A notation in the margin.

With thumb and index finger of left hand, the doctor clamped her cheeks and rotated her head from side to side. "Bilateral mid-face retrusion." Check. Efficiently, he spun away from the patient, applied the prophylactics, and turned back to insert his smooth, latex-encased fingers into Mrs. Lindstrom's small opening, gently forcing it wider against taut skin. The lack of dental support had caused the mouth to sink inward, tightening the opening, making the lips resistant to stretching. Her self-conscious habit of speaking softly through motionless lips—an effort to avoid drawing attention to that horribly shrunken slit—had only accelerated the atrophy of muscles and further shrinkage.

The doctor's fingers explored inside the lips along the gum line while Marjorie looked on, pen in hand. "Bite." Gently, he peeled away the lips to get a better view of the teeth, running his rubbered digits up under the lips, stroking the gums. Mrs. Lindstrom's eyes watered from pain and longing. "Deep impinging overbite, over-retracted upper and lower incisor profile, upper anterior teeth inclined lingually." *Pushed halfway to the uvula. The butcher!* "Lower crowding." Check, check, notation. A haphazard sprouting of lower teeth stood like young shoots pushing up from the floor of the mouth, fighting for room under the shade of a very normal, long, and lovely tongue.

He pulled out, gloved fingers wet. "Marjorie," he

said, still looking at the patient, this time into her eyes, which found his eyes briefly before her hand whisked up to push away a tear threatening to spill. "The lower ones," interrupted Mrs. Lindstrom, lips trembling. "They were straight once, when he finished the treatment."

Dr. Reckner intensified his gaze, lost everything around him but her. "I know," he started, unable to remove his eyes. *Was she out of her mind? Suddenly trying to defend the man who had "ruined" her life?* "But they've shifted over the last several years, haven't they?" She nodded in agreement. "The upper teeth have no support and they've sunk very deep. The lower teeth are pushed back, they're trapped, nowhere to go. Nowhere...," his voice trailed. Lost.

He turned away, needing a moment to find the room, his hands, his gloves. He removed them, limp and wet. He cleared his throat. "Marjorie. Do you have those x-rays from Dr. Broadhurst?" Marjorie's eyes darted up over rims of glasses. "There," she said, tipping her head toward the wall behind him. A stupid oversight! Of course, Marjorie had already pinned the x-rays on the back-lit display.

The doctor wheeled over to take a look and confirmed the suspected danger. "You see here," he pointed, becoming professorial. Mrs. Lindstrom, hair mussed and cheeks damp, pushed up awkwardly onto an elbow against the reclined back of the chair. Her eyes caught Marjorie's but quickly pulled away again, focusing on the x-ray at the end of the doctor's pointed finger, while Marjorie hastily stuffed the examination form into the folder. "There's evidence of root resorption on all four upper incisors," explained the doctor.

"Yes, Dr. Broadhurst mentioned something about that."

"The scars of orthodontia. You've lost a good third of the root structure."

"How?"

"Your teeth were moved too quickly, too..." violently, he wanted to say, "too far, too fast."

"But is it...?"

"No. It isn't. It's not too late." He was firm and adamant. A man. But on the inside, this is what the good doctor meant: *I'll help you! I'll help you, by God, I'll rectify this!*

As a very young boy, Davey loved to play with the plaster molds his father would give him from finished cases, the pre-treatment impressions. These disembodied teeth, white and crumbling, were fascinating in the seemingly infinite patterns that nature designed for a mouth. Crooked teeth, jutting teeth, crossed teeth, huge gaps, holes where teeth should have grown, pegs, all gums and no teeth, all teeth and no gums, lower jaws twice the size of uppers, cross bites, overbites, werewolf fangs, multiple rows like sharks. The most grotesque were the most exciting and awakened his need to fix them, but when he got a little older, they awakened other needs as well, giving him the idea to touch himself in their presence, doing it again and again—a memory he now liked to suppress, remembering instead the innocent games of a younger age.

He would line them up, rearrange them, mismatch a

lower jaw with someone else's upper, and even break them into sections (using his own bare hands in the years before his father allowed him a knife for that purpose). Individuals, twos, and threes, patterns mapped out on the floor of his bedroom. A ten-foot, wall-to-wall line of twelve-year molars. A circle of upper central and lateral incisors belonging to a dozen faceless kids.

Most fascinating were Davey's own teeth. The ankylosed lower bicuspid had presented his father with a most challenging problem. There was surgery to remove it, and two years of braces to fill the gap and correct the bite. These were the years, ages twelve and thirteen, when Davey began to linger in the office after his treatments, peering over his father's shoulder. In high school, he'd often walk to the office after school, interspersing home-work with informal future career education.

Dr. Reckner Sr. was a big, robust man, a commanding presence, the kind of father a son obeyed and sought to please. "David," he would say in a powerful voice (by high school, the boy was no longer "Davey"), "hand me a couple of separators. No, the posterior, not anterior." His assistant, Marjorie, easily could have helped, but she stepped out of the way, a benevolent angel overlooking the lesson, never coming between father and son.

This good, healthy curiosity about teeth seemed to run in the family, Sr. encouraging Jr.'s interest without demanding it, just as his own father had. He would talk at length about malocclusions, their many manifestations, the theory and practice of movement, torque, and union, the infinite positions on the way to a perfect fit, the means to the end. "It's an exciting process, isn't it, David?" he would say, absently tooling an elastics hemostat between index and middle fingers. "Yes, it's the process itself that's exciting."

His meaning came clear at the conclusion of every case. David saw it. The last brace was removed, and the doctor's hands would go slightly limp and spent, his mouth turned downward with sudden disinterest, not proud and beaming the way David thought it should look. Completion. A rolling over. Sleep. The next day, a virgin mouth and new interest.

At his father's office he often saw kids he knew from school, mostly girls, because even though boys' teeth were just as bad, parents were more likely to spend that kind of money on their daughters. It was there he got to know Clarissa. She began treatment her freshman year in high school, his sophomore year, but he didn't have the courage to ask her on a date until her teeth were finished, the second semester of his senior year. He made a point of knowing her schedule and never missed a visit, pretending he just happened to be around.

The doctor saw his son's interest in the girl and fully approved, maybe because the doctor himself responded well to her pleasantness and compliance, traits that reminded him of David's mother. He allowed his son to hover close behind while Clarissa was in the chair, and even made a second set of plaster impressions for David to play with early on, not waiting until the case was over.

Clarissa's God-given mouth had a buck, gap-toothed smile. Some would call it ugly, but her teen admirer kept his copy of it preserved in plaster, took care not to damage it, and stored it in a box, taking it out from time to time when he wanted to recreate that small thrill of excitement he felt the first time he'd laid eyes on her. At night, he would dream of his father's hands in her mouth, inserting instruments, twisting wires, tightening and adjusting, Clarissa's eyes darting in pain, searching for him just behind his father's shoulder, silent, rapt. He would awake in the middle of the night sweating, in a puddle of sticky wet.

Two and a half years of this, after she'd been weaned from the last retainer, David asked her out, and on their second date, worked up the courage to kiss her new mouth. It was a flawless mouth but surprisingly bland, nothing near what he'd dreamed. Pleasant, vanilla, comfortable, an immaculate fit with his, also perfect. Later that night, at home, he removed her original teeth from their box, set them on the bedside table under the blue glow of a nightlight, and stared at them until his eyelids grew heavy with sleep. He maintained this ritual for several years but was ashamed to tell Clarissa and hid the plaster teeth in the basement once they were married.

After Mrs. Lindstrom had gone, Dr. Reckner asked Marjorie for her opinion. She wasn't a doctor and hadn't the schooling, but her years of experience—eighteen with his father and twenty with him—had given her uncanny wisdom and insight.

Not intentionally had Dr. Reckner courted this family institution. His employment of Marjorie had been quite unplanned. That first day, she'd simply shown up at the door of his new practice in Piedmont, the year he'd gotten his degree and board certification, five years after his father's shocking and untimely death at the age of fifty-three from a heart attack.

Her visit came as a surprise. His last vision of Marjorie had been from a distance, out the corner of his eye at the funeral as he huddled with his mother, supporting her by the elbow. His mother barely gave the woman a glance. Understandably, Mrs. Reckner was overcome with grief, but still it was odd that, as many years as Marjorie had served the doctor, she hadn't grown closer to his family. There was no animus between the two women, but neither was there much in the way of acknowledgement. Marjorie was always in the background, even then at the funeral where she stood ten feet apart from the rest, her black clothing blacker than theirs and her face tough but puckered from secret crying. Spinster, was the word that came to David's mind, knowing he shouldn't think it.

Explaining her unexpected presence in Jr.'s office that first day, Marjorie made an uncharacteristically intimate admission. She'd been despondent ever since Sr.'s death, living frugally off her savings and the profit-sharing plan, coming dangerously close to becoming destitute, unable to bring herself to apply for another job. "I'm aware, even before looking, that other dentists and orthodontists won't measure up," she told him. "You're the closest to him, and I'd like to work again. So, I'm asking you for a job." She was willing to commute the considerable distance from her apartment in San Francisco to the outlying East Bay suburb of Piedmont. Moving from the city—the place she'd lived and worked for so many years alongside his father—was out of the question.

He wasn't quite sure how to take her. As a boy he'd seen her work. He remembered his father speaking highly of her, knew she was a superlative assistant and someone he should hire in a minute, but her surprise visit with her admitted depression and neurotic show of loyalty placed her in a new light, somewhere on the fringe. And another thing, she was looking at him in a way that said she knew him completely, at once putting him on edge and convincing him of her place in his office.

Suddenly he was reminded of a time, or times, when she'd looked at his father the same way, times when he'd been excluded. A girl would walk in, chin tucked into her neck, eyes darting from side to side, needful and scared, and Marjorie would give his father that look. Their eyes would meet, and they would exchange a little smile just before the doctor discreetly placed a hand on David's shoulder and led him out of the examining room, whispering low, "There's only so much you can do for some of these patients," closing the door behind him while Marjorie, in the background, sought to make the girl comfortable in the chair. There'd been a few cases like this, ones that, young David assumed, were beyond his ability to comprehend, or perhaps too painful for a boy to watch.

Momentarily taken by this memory, he hastily blurted a response to Marjorie's job request. "Well, I'm flattered you've taken this trouble to look me up."

"Don't be," she said. "I'm not trying to flatter you. I would like to work for you." Her sincerity was apparent.

The doctor was fascinated enough to give it a try, reminding himself he would be perfectly entitled to fire her if she couldn't meet his demands or if, perhaps, she revealed a morbid obsession with his father.

But she started right in, worked hard, needed no training, understood every wire, elastic, and retainer, never gave him a reason, personal or professional, to fire her. Even better, she was understanding and instinctively supportive of the Reckner male tradition whenever his fifteen-year-old son Bradford was around, in the same way she'd facilitated his own hands-on education in his father's office.

And so, with time, Marjorie had surpassed the position of subordinate and was now regarded as a colleague. The doctor's respect for her judgment was such that, on the day of Mrs. Lindstrom's first visit, he automatically turned to her after the patient had left and asked, "What did you think of that woman's teeth?"

Marjorie tipped her head in thought and took her time answering. "This one, I'm afraid, will be your most challenging case," she said. "A Class I+ malocclusion."

And she might have left it at that if the doctor had been satisfied and walked away. But her opinion clearly did not stop there. Dr. Reckner could see it in the way she wasn't looking at him. Marjorie was a woman who, while distant in some ways, never shrank from direct eye contact, and her difficulty in looking at him seemed to say something new—just *what* he couldn't guess. Her eyes were examining every tool on the instrument tray, as if checking each one for cleanliness. He followed her gaze and a glint stabbed his eye, a line of white light glancing off the silvery sterile hue of the ligature pliers. He felt something unspoken like an impossible, baseless intuition, and he chose to ignore it.

"Yes, challenging," he agreed. "But not impossible?"

"No, not that." Still, she didn't look up. "In some ways it might appear that way. The root structure could fail us completely, so I know you'll want to move slowly with this one." She stretched the word "slowly," making the doctor catch his breath. "But for you, not impossible."

"You have great faith."

"I only say what's true. You are your father's son." She paused as if considering whether to go on, and when she did, her voice was quiet but measured and sure. "This was—would have been—his dream case."

He nodded. He knew this.

She looked up at him then, smiled fleetingly, and dropped her eyes again. "This is the case you've been waiting for."

He knew this too.

Mrs. Lindstrom returned the following week to begin her treatment on a day when Bradford happened to be visiting his father at the office. Behind Marjorie's lead, Mrs. Lindstrom walked in from the waiting room, chin self-consciously tucked into her neck, eyes darting and needful. Dr. Reckner, explaining the different functions of needle-nose and flat-tip pliers to his son, turned around to meet Marjorie's eyes and suddenly felt a curious wave of fatherly protection and concern. No need to show Bradford just yet—such a grotesque mouth, such a difficult case, and what would be, necessarily, a painful treatment.

He glanced at Mrs. Lindstrom and his pulse quickened in the same way his own father's might have surged at the prospect of a challenging case. Had he been given the time to think, the chance to step back and observe from afar, he might have remembered this particular case. But how could he remain detached in the presence of Mrs. Lindstrom's mouth with that small tremor of fear it evoked, something the doctor instinctively defined as a proper concern for his son? Not good to let Bradford remain. No need to discourage the boy so soon from the high practice of orthodontics. He nodded to Marjorie, who escorted Mrs. Lindstrom to the chair while he put an arm around the boy's shoulder and gently steered him into his office, suggesting that he finish his homework.

He took the stool and wheeled up close. Mrs. Lindstrom was willing to go all the way, to do whatever the doctor wished, but still she had many questions. The doctor explained the need for full braces, upper and lower, to be worn for a lengthy period of time because he would have to proceed with caution, applying only the gentlest pressure to avoid further damage to the root system, to preserve teeth whose integrity was threatened by bone loss, receding gums, and blunted roots.

"How long?" she asked, already settled into the examination chair, looking as if she belonged there. She wore a dark, long-sleeved turtleneck dress of a soft knit fabric, something that clung to her body, outlining it against the beige upholstery of the chair. He looked down and saw he would have to cover it.

"Lift," said the doctor, indicating her head. She did as he said, jutting her head forward, ready for the paper bib for her upper body. Covering it. He affixed the clasp around her neck. "Hard to say," he replied to her question. "Usual treatment time is about eighteen months. In your case, it will be longer." His left hand lingered briefly on her shoulder. "At least two years, maybe two and a half or three." He would see how it went with her. He would see from month to month what he needed to do inside her mouth.

"Marjorie," said the doctor loudly to drown out the noise in his head, but his assistant was just behind him, looking down into Mrs. Lindstrom's hole. Fumbling with latex gloves, the doctor wasn't aware, but there was another look from Marjorie over his shoulder, away from that mouth, up into the patient's eyes, a look that was greeted and reciprocated and understood.

"It's been a long time," said Mrs. Lindstrom, still looking at Marjorie. The doctor, oblivious, slid inside, pushing her open.

"Yes, yes, just relax. Marjorie, I'll start with a 16."

His assistant found the requested item in her large plastic tray with dozens of inch-square compartments for metal bands of every size, for every tooth. The doctor took the one she handed him, positioned it on a back molar, pushed, found his rubber hammer on the table, tapped it down. A perfect fit. Later he would remove it, apply the cement, tap it down again for permanence.

"14."

Marjorie handed it, he positioned, pushed, pushed

again harder, tapped. He stopped to consider his next move, and the patient spoke. "Your hands are like his," she said, making him pull away, startled. "So sure," she explained. "At least, they seemed sure at the time, but they were doing the wrong thing, weren't they?"

"Yes, that doctor." He busied his hands again. "Marjorie, I need another 14. That nameless doctor in, where did you say?"

"San Francisco."

"Yes, a big town, many orthodontists. Don't worry, Mrs. Lindstrom. I'm doing the right thing here."

Blind and deaf, he ignored the clues, feeling only annoyance at this interruption of his work. He didn't want her to speak any more. He wouldn't give her the chance. He positioned each band, pushed and hammered and kept going, one tooth after another for an hour and a half, cemented each one, applied brackets on two uppers and two lowers, threaded the wire, pinched and tweaked it with the flat-tip pliers, inserted elastics with the grooved hemostat, and used the twist-on to place the elastic ligature ties. All the while, he glanced now and then at her eyes, closed and drawn tight against the pain, tears squeezed out the sides, nostrils flared and cheeks in high color from the pushing and pulling inside her mouth.

Was this the kind of pain he saw in every face, in all his patients? He'd always regretted it, or thought he had, but with her there was no regret, only necessity, certainty, drive. Every atom of her face was exposed under the light, the crease between her eyes deepening inside those delicate accordions of brows pushed up tight together over the bridge of her nose as she and the doctor came closer and closer, nearing completion. She couldn't speak, wasn't allowed to, couldn't possibly have uttered a word as he worked and worked on her, probed, pushed, and pulled deep inside that mouth.

But what was that coming from her throat? He heard it, a word grunted between needful breaths. *Tighter.* And again. *Tighter.*

At last, they reached the end. He wiped his brow, his hands trembling as he removed the gloves. He was aware at once of his breathing, his pulse, the quickness. But he was finished with Mrs. Lindstrom. For now. There would be many other times.

He rolled back from the patient on his stool and instinctively swiveled around to look up at Marjorie. This time, her eyes did not shy away from direct contact. Her face was content, filled with a maternal glow, the benevolent look of a proud guardian. The facilitator of something good, something exciting, something her son needed, especially now at this stage of his career, at this stage of middle life.

And all at once, Dr. Reckner saw it. He knew what her expression conveyed, and he accused her silently.

He did this, didn't he?

The glow of pride, the slightest of smiles.

My father! He destroyed this woman's mouth!

With his eyes he penetrated Marjorie, hoping to see something else in that unchanging countenance as a persistent thought played again and again in his mind. *He did this for me! He sent her to me!*

Stunned, he dropped his eyes to the floor. Marjorie's face, that single look, had shattered all his carefully laid images of his father. Still, in the midst of his profound shock, he felt the gradual swelling of enormous awe. What genius! The timing of it, so perfect, a glacial, twenty-five-year collapse of dental health.

He turned to look up again at Marjorie. "How could this...? When?" He searched her eyes for the answer.

Marjorie's face was at once transformed, becoming businesslike. "Would you say about four weeks, Doctor?" she asked, picking up the file and a pen to make a notation.

"Yes," interrupted Mrs. Lindstrom, pushing herself up, dazed and heavy-lidded from pain. "I can barely speak," she panted and smiled. "About every four weeks, isn't that it? The usual time between appointments?"

The doctor spun around to behold her, and she returned his stare, mouth pink and battered, lips slightly swollen from all the tugging and pulling. Fuller, almost pretty. Her eyes, so familiar, knew exactly what she was about, who he was and why she was here. Forgot the name! Mrs. Lindstrom had come looking for him, for what she needed, and what she needed she would be getting right here, in this chair. Instantly, the doctor lost any fear of consequence. He could see that his father had chosen the right one, had chosen well. A gift from father to son.

"Yes, four weeks," said Dr. Reckner. The days in between would be their time to recover, to envision, to anticipate.

She stood up, and with a small wobble, was on her heels and gone.

A sudden hush enveloped the examining room, now

with only the doctor and Marjorie and the chair and the instruments. Other patients couldn't be seen, but they could be felt outside the door in the waiting room sitting restlessly, reading magazines. Bradford sat behind the closed door of the doctor's office, innocently doing his homework. Dr. Reckner walked to that door and stopped, hand on the knob, suddenly unable to face his son, not knowing what to say, unable to envision anything normal coming from his mouth.

"Doctor?"

It seemed now that he'd been standing immobile for quite some time. It was apparent in Marjorie's tone. At once, the certainty and strength he'd felt when looking down into the patient's eyes dissolved into nothingness.

"What am I to do with this woman?" he whispered, not turning to face his assistant.

"You will do what you do for every case, for every one of your patients."

Yes, this is what he did for his patients, for every one. Relied on his judgment, wisdom, and experience, used his best efforts, applied every tactical consideration, every innovative procedure, gave of himself one hundred percent toward one goal: to fix the malocclusion. He'd always been proud of that. With Mrs. Lindstrom, he would remind himself to indulge that professional pride, would convince himself of its legitimacy despite these other, messy things that were, after all, merely visceral and hidden.

His son waited. He started to turn the knob.

"There may be others," he heard at his back.

∭FRACTALS

MINERVA THRIEBOLD IS a tenured professor in the mathematics department of a formerly women's (now coed) private liberal arts college in New England. Isabella Baggio is one of three backup singers for a popular male entertainer on the cruise ship circuit and lives in Miami when stateside.

At the age of four, Minerva developed a dislike for her name and methodically repositioned the letters into every possible combination of seven, six, and five letters. She settled on Verna and proclaimed it. Her parents, Lucy and Brill, did not resist, although Minerva had been named after Lucy's favorite grandmother. Years later, Lucy was throwing out old toys when she found Verna's name combinations on a piece of paper wadded inside Mr. Potato Head's hat. In that childish handwriting, Lucy discerned a foreshadowing of mathematical genius, a grasp of algorithm.

Isabella, from the time she was an infant, was known as Bebe, a nickname created from the two b's in her names. Her mother, Sharyn, reflexively adopted the pet name during an episode of gentle cooing with her newborn. "Isabella Baggio, b – b – b – b!" she repeated, making a sound that put a smile on the baby's face and seemed to capture her sunny, sweet disposition. The spelling was later simplified to "bb" after the fashion of ee cummings, the mother's favorite poet.

In 1969, Verna and bb were sixteen. In 2004, they are both fifty-one. Verna and her husband Kent have been together for twenty-four years and have two teenagers, a girl and a boy. bb is, and always has been, single.

If their lives were the subject of a simple geometry lesson, they might be two lines in a plane, not parallel, required to intersect once, never to meet again.

"A fractal is a fragmented geometric shape we can split into parts which are each a reduced copy of the whole. This is a property called self-similarity." Verna moves the mouse and clicks, projecting an image of a romanesco onto the screen in the dark classroom. The olive-green vegetable, a cross between broccoli and cauliflower, displays the pleasing symmetry of repeating pattern. "Fractals, or approximations of them, occur in nature, like this romanesco."

Verna is not entirely present in her lecture. This morning she received an e-mail on her office computer at the college, a big surprise that, in the abstract, should have been interesting and exciting. But the intervening decades have marked the sender, imbuing her message with an aftertaste. Verna is left feeling sad and resentful, beset by involuntary thoughts. *Too little too late. Go away.*

Lines of sun pierce the closed Venetian blinds in the

classroom. Seduced by the muted light, she intones, "A mathematical fractal is generated by an equation that undergoes iteration, endless feedback based on recursion. Can anyone think of an example of infinite recursion?"

An eager male hand shoots up in the gray. She points. "A spiral, infinitely winding into the center," he suggests, more or less sure of himself.

"Not always. It depends."

Another hand goes up. "Mirrors facing each other," says a girl. "The reflection inside a reflection inside a…"

"…reflection, inside a reflection inside a…" The class takes up the chant for several iterations and dissolves into laughter, a surrender to impulse driven by the fresh, April afternoon seeping in through the slats.

Professor Thriebold, for all her gravity, is known to allow, on occasion, a complete youthful surrender to the beauty of math. She laughs along and forgets.

Lucille Mae Fish grew up on a farm in Ohio, and Edward Brill Thriebold was the son of a San Francisco surgeon and a wealthy Nob Hill socialite. Lucy and Brill met while undergraduates at the University of California, and upon their graduation in 1951, both just twenty-two, they married and chose to make their home in Berkeley, where they raised their only child Minerva, born in 1953.

That quiet, pale girl with dirty-blonde hair and full-moon eyes lived her life from infanthood to the age of fourteen immersed in the soothing self-satisfaction of textbook learning. She was at the top of her class, master of the pop quiz, multiple-choice, and standardized test, a natural leader of the "smart" group in a time when pedagogues were not trained to conceal the intellectual differences among children.

Verna did not shun her classmates, but neither did she seek them out. She was too socially insecure to be forward but always had a friend or two, never as smart and without anything else about them sufficiently intriguing to make up for it. This is how it was, until bb came along.

It was 1967, the Summer of Love. In an unknown, faraway place, the recently divorced Sharyn Baggio assumed a new identity, "Zenith," and journeyed with a younger man into that brewing explosion of a town Berkeley, bringing along her two girls, bb and eleven-year-old Ernestina. Zenith's new lover had swept her away with his dream of making a pilgrimage to the epicenter of Flower Power. He didn't come to participate in peaceful antiwar demonstrations but to experience the move-ment's tantalizing offshoot, the credo, "turn on, tune in, drop out." The man's name was Ray.

On April 6, 2004, Isabella sits in the light-filled, pastel-colored living room of her modest bungalow ten blocks from Miami Beach when a name pops into her head. She believes the name might have meant something to her at one time, but it has faded into the file of forgotten regrets and died with that part of her she successfully buried and laid to molder, fertilizing the greater, stronger part she's coaxed up to the surface, the part that has survived. There is no one left to recognize the traces of death that remain at the core of her being because her sunny side has been reborn, blooming up from the decay.

The familiar name percolates to the top with a cheery sort of, "I wonder whatever happened to...?" She goes to her desk and lets her fingers wander to the Internet browser where she finds Minerva Thriebold, a woman who has kept her full maiden name as her professional name, a professor of mathematics. Isabella understands the words on her screen to represent a valid identity, the larger projection of the smaller girl of sixteen she once knew. She explores the college website, finds the e-mail address for Professor Thriebold, and sends a thrilled, heartfelt message, replete with exclamation points. She refrains, however, from adding a happy face.

The Summer of Love, for Verna, meant its opposite, the beginning of a three-year bumpy escalation to the end of her parents' marriage. She was witness to restrained squalls with frustrated grabs and shoving, followed by sickly sweet reconciliations. Stone cold silences. Political arguments, Lucy the rational, cautious one, Brill the socialist firebrand. They would forget about their child and then suddenly remember, acknowledging her existence with guilty, darting eyes.

At one time, their love had been overpowering. Lucy made a huge statement when she left a life of corn ears and alfalfa to follow her intellectual dreams to a distant university where she committed herself to a man with a socially unfamiliar past. Lucy and Brill's differences and their shared pursuit of careers in social research were enough to bind them inseparably against the tug of family roots.

But then the '60s took hold, and Brill became ever

more strident and anti-establishment and resentful of his own easy beginnings, angry and ashamed of his parents' wealth. Lucy reacted, retreating into her mind, into the past and the tranquility of wind-blown acres of grain, family meals around the oak table, fundamental values, respect.

Verna escaped into her books and couldn't wait for the summer to be over and her freshman year at Berkeley High School to begin. On that September morning at 8:00 a.m., she walked into first period English and chose one of the tottering wood desks in the back row. She usually sat in the front where she could receive her academic due, but her behavior had started to show the signs of a new insecurity, the creeping influence of family strife. Her choice of seat that day was provident, for bb plunked down in the wobbling desk next to hers in the back.

Mr. McGraff had not yet opened his mouth when bb timidly glanced at Verna, dared to hold her eyes, and suddenly broke out in a smile, an intense flash of meridian light. "Hi!!!" she bubbled with her voice full of exclamation points, as it always was and always would be.

With one look, Verna guessed the new girl was a C-plus student. It didn't matter. Of greater interest were bb's unknowable past and her enigmatic arrival. The attraction was mutual, a simultaneous desire for outlet, to speak of everything except what must be forgotten and supposed not to exist, and here they were, magically sitting together, finding each other in the exact moment of need.

There could be no doubt as to bb's sincerity. The

proof was in her physical beauty, which far surpassed Verna's plain features, a disparity that established the certainty of their deeper affinity. bb was the poster-lovechild hippie with waist-length ebony hair in full natural curl, wearing patched bellbottoms and a raw-edged, leather fringe vest over raglan-sleeved paisley. Her smile carried the promise of sublime love and beauty, transcendence.

Verna was taken. From that day forward, they were inseparable.

Lucy and Brill were so completely immersed in their own misery they hardly noticed Verna's increasing absence and the changes in her behavior. Her grades never suffered. School had become somewhat too easy for her and home life somewhat too difficult, leaving a void to be filled.

bb lived just five blocks away. Verna started following her home after school, sometimes to stay, sometimes to stop off on their way to bigger adventures. She came to know every crack and assaultive weed in the concrete walkway leading to that small single-story in the Berkeley flats. A choking screen of overgrown bushes obscured the front door. Directly inside that door was a cramped living room in plum and mustard colors, the air often thick with the marijuana and cigarette smoke of long-haired men who slouched over congas and guitars, their long-haired women skulking in the shadows, attached to cow bells or tambourines.

To the right was a narrow hallway leading to three tiny bedrooms and a bathroom, and straight through the living room was the kitchen with its pungent odor of tanned cowhide. The grimy countertops and dinette table brimmed with the tools, raw materials, and wares of Ray's leather business, Stingray Designs: fringe vests, belts, and Confederate rebel hats. Leftover signs of the munchies would be strewn about, baking tins with crusted brownie residue or blackened pots with an inch of cold stew.

The first time up the front walkway, as Verna was swallowed by the bushes hiding the secret door, a flash of panic hit. This was her first impulsive act of rebellion, an after-school visit she hadn't revealed to her parents. That day, the living room held three men. Leading Verna through, bb cast a shade of dark curls down over her eyes as if she might, in this way, make it into the kitchen without being noticed. A man's voice, forced and silky, came up from the floor where he was sitting cross-legged on the dirty shag carpet with a guitar resting in the deep diamond between knees and crotch.

"Little flower," he said. "Made a new friend at school?" One of the men glanced at the girls with sleepy eyes, the other was stuffing a bong.

bb stopped and turned. "This is Verna," she announced to the room with her sunny smile, avoiding his eyes.

The inquiring man regarded Verna, letting his gaze slip here and there, finally settling on her face. Her eyes grew wide and he laughed. "She tell you who I am? bb can forget her manners." His hair seemed wet or maybe greasy, combed close to his head, ending in snakelike waves at the bottom of his neck. His blue eyes, closer to gray in the dim room, were gripping, mesmerizing.

"This is Ray," said bb.

"Isabella's stepdad," he corrected, and waved his hand to shoo them away. "Go on, baby munchkins, and get some cookies and milk."

Verna gladly followed her friend out of that living room and into the kitchen, where they scrounged for a snack within the morass of leather pouches and sandals bearing imprints of peace signs, yins and yangs. The refrigerator held a few cans of beer, ketchup and relish, a single bagless hotdog roll.

"Doesn't your stepdad have to go to work?"

"He makes all this stuff at home." bb laughed and twirled in a circle, letting her Indian cotton dress balloon and settle again on her slim, braless form. Verna felt instantly comfortable to be with another girl as flat as herself in a room away from the prying eyes of men and boys. "Bitchen!" Verna said, trying bb's favorite word.

"Yeah. And then he tries to sell it on the weekends."

"Far out! Your stepdad is pretty cool." The words spilled automatically, like an obligation.

bb smiled vacantly and said nothing, her face a picture of studied absence deep within. Verna couldn't understand that look, but it made her regret what she'd just said. In time, she would figure out that Zenith was the breadwinner, allowing Ray to falter and b.s. at the flea markets where he bartered his wares for a high or netted a few coins after expenses.

bb rummaged in a cabinet. "Here, you want this?" She smiled brightly and held out a box of Cocoa Puffs, but her little sister Tina appeared from nowhere and laid claim: "Hey, mine!"

bb held the box up in the air and demanded, "Give

me a hug first! Come on and give me a hug!" As Tina came for it, bb lunged, picked the girl up, and spun her around in a dazzling burn of love! Where did all this love come from? It exploded in a burst of hard brown pebbles onto the floor!

Just as quickly, bb dropped her sister and the box and took Verna's hand to lead her away while Tina scrambled for the sugary bits on the floor. They escaped to bb's room and shut the door. It would be their cocoon, a cozy squeeze on all sides with the paisley bedspread tacked to the ceiling in air-filled scallops and the walls covered with posters of the Doors, Beatles, Rolling Stones, and Grateful Dead.

They spent the afternoon applying mascara and eyeliner while Verna answered bb's questions about certain kids at school. Later, bb put the Sgt. Pepper LP on a pink turntable and started to sing in a voice that was full, clear, pure, and easy. Verna joined in. She had but one artistic love, and that was the study of music, mostly classical. She played the piano and loved to sing and could hold a tune but struggled to listen to herself, to make sure she didn't go sharp. Whenever she became worried about losing pitch, her volume would plummet to near nothingness.

There was no such worry that afternoon as her voice rode on the stronger current by her side. She dreamed of timeless music—hymns, madrigals, and chorales—and by the end of the afternoon, she'd convinced her new friend to join A Cappella, an after-school club.

"Fractals are infinitely complex. Take this one, for

example. You see it here as I zoom in at different levels of magnification. In the next few weeks, we'll explore some of the techniques for generating fractals: iterated function systems, both deterministic and non-deterministic, random fractals, escape-time fractals. Strange attractors."

The slide collage devolves into a fast-paced light show as Verna clicks on image after image, a fern, a cloud, a crystal, a Koch snowflake, cauliflower, mountain range, river network, branching pulmonary vessels, tree limbs, a fractal flame like wispy smoke. The flashing images take her back. She sits again on that long, slick seat in the boat-like Chevrolet, pushed up against the passenger door, Zenith driving, bb center, the three of them bumping and sliding in the dark toward red taillights and green traffic lights smudged on a rainy windshield. She strangles on smoke from Zenith's cigarettes, and now the burning roach is passed from mother to daughter, and from daughter to daughter's friend, click, click, click, a Sierpinski triangle, Mandelbrot set, chaos game—color, angle, pattern, shape, infinity, vortex. They step into the Fillmore in San Francisco and push through an intermittent, strobe-lit crowd of tie-dye in a cavernous space, walled in splashing colors. They twitch and undulate, a thousand separate souls immersed in the rasping anger of Janis Joplin.

Wait! Where did they go? Pressed on all sides, Verna is surrounded and alone, stripped of bb's love, Zenith's protection. Dizzy and paranoid, a pinprick of light, she pushes through the squirming bodies, halts, and circles. Fright chokes her neck, wobbles her knees. Why would anyone want to feel like this, to be in a place like this?

There? No. There! "bb!" And as she yells out, voiceless in the din, Zenith's arms reach up from behind. Verna turns and looks down into the face of the petite woman with the deep, sensitive eyes and accepts her embrace. In her ear she feels the startling, husky voice.

"Verna."

> "My goodness, Verna, this must be you! You were so smart—I always knew you would make it to the top! Do you remember me? From way back when, Berkeley High? I live in Miami now, but most of the time I work on cruise ships. I'm a vocalist! Remember A Cappella? Please write. I'd love to know how you're doing! Maybe we could get together sometime and catch up?
>
> "Luv, Isabella"

Her finger moves to "send" but remains frozen. The missive isn't complete. Again, she poises herself to type but stops, feeling the sudden sting of a buried dagger. Internal training takes hold, the deep breathing sets in. She waits it out. *There now. My gosh, how ridiculous!*

> "P.S. You might remember me as 'bb,' but I don't use that name anymore!!!"

As freshman year wore on, they talked endlessly about boys and pretended to hope, yet knew, that they would never have boyfriends. bb was so beautiful it puzzled

Verna that a boy hadn't taken her away. At the same time, it was unthinkable because there wasn't an inch of space between them to allow anyone else in. The only time they were apart was late at night.

They suspected that sex was prevalent within a certain set of their classmates. This was not said bluntly but expressed with eye contact and suggestion. "Free love" was the standard, and it came to hang a weight around their necks.

Verna was secretly convinced of a societal expectation that she lose her virginity as soon as possible. The absurdity of this, for a girl of fourteen, was not apparent to her. Embarrassed to admit it, she had overheard her parents making love, less so in recent times. First on her "to do" list was calculus homework, last was sex, right underneath cleaning her room, but on the list nevertheless.

There were no rules, advice, or guidance from her parents, but just as well, because she couldn't possibly discuss this subject with them. Imagining that bb and Zenith had long, female conversations, she was jealous. Zenith was so unlike other mothers. She would coolly suggest their next adventure, mysterious and unknowable behind her cigarette smoke and gray-green eyes, slivered in a protective squint with every drag. Surely bb was able to talk to her, and maybe Verna could too, if she needed to talk, but she'd convinced herself of no such need. The facts and evidence of expectation and obligation were unavoidable, blazoned on the face of the world.

Zenith had a fulltime clerk-typist job and was never home during the day. The three of them were together only on their special Saturday nights when Ray was off at some other house jamming. Those were the evenings filled with dense smoke, swimming heads, pounding music, and trips to Denny's at three a.m. Tina was considered too young to come along. Verna wasn't quite sure where she stayed on those nights.

In A Cappella they were learning "Ode to Joy," Beethoven's 9th. On the few occasions they went to Verna's house, she would play the record and they would sing what they'd learned, knowing that it could never be as great. Everything had a gap between real and imagined—free love too—that was what Verna suspected. She couldn't ask bb outright what she believed about sex, afraid of the probable response, a sunny smile with an "outasite!" Afraid, maybe, that bb would say she'd actually done it, as impossible as it was.

They were not supposed to be self-conscious about the outlines of their own bare nipples poking through the cloth as they observed more dramatic development under the blouses of their classmates. They dropped joking hints about their endless wait, and as it turned out, they would keep waiting forever. Their bodies were alike in this way, but what did it matter to bb, who was so completely beautiful? In candlelight and incense, they styled each other's hair and took turns running the brush bristles along bared arms and backs to feel the exciting tickle.

Often enough, Verna suggested they go to her house, but they usually ended up at bb's. She wasn't sure why. There was an invisible pull. Ray would be in the living room nearly every afternoon, jamming and smoking.

They would receive his sidelong look or a "munchkin" comment on their way to bb's room.

Only once did he walk into their secret sanctum without knocking. bb did not utter a protest, but a small ripple of emotion passed through her body.

"Lady Guinevere. Tell me your secrets!"

He closed the door behind him and sat on the bed next to bb. She scooted away an inch, stoking his attention. The dilated pupils in his glittering eyes pulled their space into his trip on something stronger than pot. A hand went to bb's shoulder, and she gave an embarrassed laugh. He massaged her neck, took up a curl on his finger, and wound himself into it, staring at her profile. "Ray!" she said under her breath with another little laugh. Verna was on the floor by the turntable looking through a stack of records, averting her eyes, feeling hot and unsure.

"What's the trippy news from Berkeley High?" he asked, drawling the last word.

"Not much."

"That singing club you go to. Sing me something." The lock was coiled around his finger, and her head tilted slightly toward him under the pressure.

Verna's senses perked. She sat up, shifting from the side of her thigh onto her knees.

"We haven't really learned anything," said bb.

"Oh, you have, I've heard you!" He was unwinding the hair now, releasing the pressure, so maybe it was nothing after all, but Verna's accelerating heart wouldn't slow down. She jumped up and began to sing "Ode to Joy"! Ray turned suddenly and dropped his hand as if taken by surprise to see her there in the room with them.

bb sprang up and joined her. Their voices swelled, obliterating the threat of bad karma, becoming stronger together, bright and clear as Ray lost edge and substance. Smiling vaguely, he listened for a while, then stood up with a slight pitch to the side and left the room.

It takes several days. She fights with herself about responding, but knows that she will, perhaps must. How can she not? How can she fail to release even a tiny bit of what would have been a gush, an open torrent of relief, anger, and love that would have been impossible to stanch thirty years ago, or even twenty? The tread of time has diminished the relief, anger, and love to just anger and love and then anger and then resentment and then a dull ache and then indifference.

But respond she does, in a middle-aged voice that neither of them ever could have foreseen, choked with suppression and filled with little white lies that maybe bb—no, Isabella—won't be able to detect in her new, apparently oblivious and incomprehensibly distant persona which so nakedly refuses to take responsibility.

"Isabella, How interesting to hear from you. Good for you, that you've been able to take up a career in singing."

She almost adds, "to make use of your talent in this way," but she can't go that far, to be so hideously hypocritical! A cruise ship!

"As you can see, I'm a professor of mathematics. It has been an enjoyable and fulfilling career."

At this point, a word or two about her family might be appropriate, but she can't bring herself to involve Kent and the children. There's nothing in Isabella's note about her own family. And so, she just ends it.

"Thank you for your note.

"Best regards, Verna"

In June of 1968, the country was reeling from two assassinations. As freshman year came to a close, Verna was looking forward to a summer of secret rendezvous with bb and Zenith, trips to be-ins and rock concerts and volunteer work for the UFW. In a private meeting, Verna's father had approved the part of the plan that included pamphleteering and picketing with the Mexican farm workers. In those days, Lucy and Brill were never in the same room at the same time. Separately, they had each met Verna's closest friend but seemed unaware of her importance.

On the morning of the last day of school, after Brill had gone to work, Lucy announced, "We're leaving on Saturday."

Verna was eating a slice of wheat berry toast. She kept chewing, unable to see her mother's face due to an involuntary habit of tilting her head down, a subconscious acknowledgement of shame. "Leaving?"

"We're going to Ohio, to visit my sister and your cousins."

Her chest tightened. Once, when she was nine, they'd gone to visit Aunt Denise, Uncle George, Kathy and Hank, the most boring people in the world on the loneliest, most expansive stretch of big-sky farmland she'd ever seen.

"Without your father," Lucy added.

"When're we coming back?"

"Not sure."

"A week?"

"Oh, longer than that. We'll be gone for some time."

That piece of toast, the good, nutty taste of it, was seared in memory, a contradiction.

That afternoon in bb's room, there was dramatic hugging and sobbing, wild plans of running away, and hopeless wailing at the futility of it. They made promises to write and to think of each other every minute of every day they were apart. And they would, and they did.

Verna didn't know that the Ohio days of 1968 were to stretch into the whole summer, a planned, trial separation between Lucy and Brill. Not aware of this, Verna remained frantic for only a few days in the beginning, then gradually succumbed to the oddly calming effect of the big sky. Tractors and acres of corn. Mashed potatoes and tumblers of frothy milk. The farm stand. Hank and experiments with French kissing. They agreed it wasn't really incest because Hank was Uncle George's boy from a previous marriage, but the taboo was great enough to restrain them from doing anything more.

Most special were the afternoons sitting alone under a huge willow, reading bb's letters. They arrived once a week, those impossible-to-fold stacks of paper rolled and shoved into business-size envelopes. In cheap blue ballpoint, the handwriting was large and round and open and uniformly slanted, neatly resting on each line of both sides of the wide-ruled binder paper. If Verna had been blind, she could have read the lines with her fingers, tracing deep impressions of passionate prose etched into the pulp.

"Oh Verna! We saw the People yesterday in Golden Gate Park and they sang 'I Love You'!!! It was so bitchen!!!"

and

"Where does the universe end???"

and

"Do they have cows and pigs where you are?"

and

"I'm lying on my back in bed counting the paisleys. I'm up to 279!!!"

That calm feeling under the big sky was owed in part to her unshakeable belief that bb was in that little house on the Berkeley flats, waiting for her to come home.

Not long after sending the reply e-mail, Verna receives a letter. Instantly, she's transported back to the farm. The paper is different, ecru stationery bearing the logo of a cruise line, but the quality of the pen and the handwriting have not changed. Childish, round, and careful, a rejection of darkness and maturity, the finite components of a complex, reiterative pattern.

"Dear Verna, It was so great to hear from you!!! Is this crazy? In May I'll be working a cruise line with a stop in Boston!"

So, the suggestion is laid. Verna might resist, might dwell in false analogy to geometric principle, concluding that a second meeting is impossible. Instead, she resigns herself immediately to their unavoidable reunion and launches into the business of its arrangement. The diversion is enough to keep her mind away from a suspicion that she still harbors a lingering, hidden yearning to lash out.

Verna returned from Ohio a week before the first day of sophomore year. The homecoming was as dramatic and tearful as the parting. Children of today might not understand. An overwhelming fear will take hold in anticipation of hearing a voice again, coming eye-to-eye again, after months of physical and vocal separation and endless days of hanging in reverie on a written exchange. A sudden realization! Freed from the inhibition of physical presence, eye contact, and body language, the flow of thought had been unleashed. She remembered all those things she'd written to bb this summer. Confessions about Hank. Descriptions of the fights between her mother and father. Dreams of becoming the greatest mathematician of all time. Envy of bb's hair and eyes.

With trepidation, Verna telephoned and froze up at the sudden intimacy of bb's voice in her ear. Nervously they made arrangements, an immediate meeting, and bb was waiting out on the sidewalk in front of her house as Verna rounded the corner. Their eyes locked and they ran, each taking her own half of the block at a sprint, and they flew into each other's arms!

Another year together had begun, in many ways similar to the last, but changed by the aura of growing unrest in the nation, the accumulation of unpleasant knowledge in their young minds, the temptation of false gratification, the glorification of anarchy, the oppression of too much freedom. Their experiments were deeper, darker, more dangerous and exciting. Verna suffered from doubt every time, before and after. They hitchhiked. They talked to strangers in the park. They smoked pot without parental supervision and snorted coke with. Zenith taught them how. They laughed and cried and felt every wonderful soaring emotion of adolescence, the panicky passion of complete inseparability.

Yet a transparent veil of inhibition separated them. Verna could see something on the other side but did not understand her friend any better. She was too busy hiding from herself, unable to utter the most painful thing. From the day of her return, it was clear that the summer apart had done little to mend her parents' relationship. bb also was hiding, leaving Verna uneasy and ignorant of how she could take the painful journey behind bb's eyes which, often, did not smile with her mouth but opened into a vast, impenetrable obliteration. Perhaps Verna's eyes said the same.

The girls covered up their secret unknowns with a mask of teen exuberance. Still, they were able to feel the depth of their souls in each other, sharing something beyond words.

A week before she takes to the sea, Isabella receives a letter. She's overjoyed to get it, not put off in the least by the businesslike tone. *My goodness, Verna was always so organized!* There's a date, a time, and a place for their reunion. An adventure! So neatly planned.

Isabella glows with a smile that's more or less permanent under the influence of countless swaying performances in eveningwear, singing the backup fragments, with innuendo, to "I Heard it Through the Grapevine." The men often look at her as they sit at tables covered in white linen, so handsome and safe, holding hands with sweethearts or wives or paramours while they allow her to smile at them from her diaphanous perch, beautiful and distant.

Since that day, a month ago, when she sent off that e-mail on a whim, a few things have come back slowly, especially some of the emotions she felt when Verna, so long ago, went off across the country, leaving her behind with…him. Twice, a summer and a year.

What, really, did she feel about Verna then? What does she feel now? She's never been angry at another person in her life, but if it's anger or betrayal, or anything else that requires forgiveness, she must have forgiven it by now. Yes, that must be it, but when? On a date uncertain, a sunny day before the sunny day that Verna's name suddenly came to mind, free and clear.

Now there's no threat of a bad feeling to swallow her up. No isolation. No fear. No self-hatred. No panic. Just a blinding white light. And something to look forward to—a new adventure for two old ladies!!!

On an afternoon in May of their sophomore year, Verna and bb cut class and went to the university campus where they stretched out on the green and made daisy chains. Mascara and daisies were bb's trademarks, thick black lashes and a halo of flowers nestled in the cushion of lustrous curls.

Although Brill and Lucy both worked at the university, Verna had the impression they didn't know of her wanderings to the campus during school hours. And if Zenith and Ray were aware of bb's playing hooky, they weren't the kind of parents to do anything about it.

That day, something was up, they could feel it. The California Highway Patrol was in town. They'd ducked a few officers on the way to campus, but their route hadn't taken them through the area of greatest concentration. In the background, they heard a voice over a loudspeaker in Sproul Plaza.

The sun shone oddly through the black coating on bb's lashes as she gazed down at the flowers in her hands. "Did you hear about People's Park?" she asked Verna.

Brill, in one of his moments of parental instruction, had spoken of it with shining eyes when Lucy wasn't around. Verna both liked and disliked him when he got like that. His energy and zeal were catching, but his absorption in what he was saying removed him to another universe. The citizenry of Berkeley, he told her, had claimed a bit of university property, where they'd planted shrubs and flowers, creating a park. There was governmental resistance. This was the part that excited Brill the most.

Verna repeated this bit of information and asked bb, "D'you think that's what they're talking about?"

Her friend jumped up and reached down to grab her arm. "Come on!"

When they got to the plaza, they pushed in at the

outskirts of a huge crowd a moment before the speaker cried out, "Let's take the park!" Verna's pounding heart was climbing high in her chest when, suddenly, they were swept up and carried away, two flies on the elephant's tail. A single being of muscle and throat and hair pushed out onto Telegraph Avenue, chanting "We want the park! We want the park!"

Their girlish voices combined with the rest, and in those first moments, the intoxication of purpose gripped Verna with a pride she'd never felt before, to be marching alongside college students with intellect and just cause, and now, wouldn't they—she caught herself—wouldn't *he*, wouldn't her *father* really be proud of his daughter! This unspoken admission declared itself within the jostle of strangers surrounding her, breaking it loose. She was surprised to discover a need for him exclusively, not for her mother who already loved her, of that she was sure. Lucy had been the one to take her away while he stayed behind, without protest, and then said so very little when they returned. He didn't really love her. No, he did not.

But the beauty and righteousness of the moment very quickly turned ugly and rotten with fear. A block ahead of them, at the front of the crowd, a swarm of uniformed officers in riot gear bore down on them, wielding bats and cocking rifles as their captain made demands by megaphone. This was no demonstration but the beginning of a melee. The students were picking up whatever came handy, a book, a rock, a bottle, even garbage out of a receptacle, taunting and threatening to hurl these things.

The girls stopped dead and turned to each other.

bb's eternal smile hovered like a ghost keeping company with the stubborn vacancy in her eyes, something familiar. Verna felt the shock of a new thought without having time to connect, to understand, to remember when she might have seen that look in her friend's eyes before. At this moment they had to act, to be in it or out of it as they found themselves uncomfortably close to the ugliest things that seemed about to happen. "Pigs!" she heard. People were on rooftops throwing things down. A scuffle broke out. An officer brought down a bat.

The girls stood immobile, trapped in ice. Verna's eyes inched left and right, and then she saw him, a man who looked like her own father and was, in fact, her own father. He pulled his arm back like a baseball pitcher and let something fly at a policeman, who deflected it with his riot shield, making a noise she could distinguish even within this ruckus. The noise of her father's rock was the loudest noise of every noise that combined in the mix of decibels making up this hell. The sound of his rock said violence like no other rock, and she wanted none of it.

Canisters shot out from the bank of cops, catching the sun, exploding in acrid plumes of smoke. Brill was caught in a cloud and he whirled, clutching his eyes, twisting blindly in circles. He threw his hands down, looked up, and started to run wildly, dodging an officer in pursuit. He was headed straight toward her. Could he see anything through the sting in his eyes?

Gunfire sounded.

"Let's go!" They turned their backs on People's Park and broke into a sprint, heading west, toward the bay.

Later, they found out that a man on the roof had

been shot and killed.

How dare she appear out of nowhere like this.

Verna is on her way to the coffee shop, fighting the desire to turn back. Her impulse is to drive to her office where she can be completely alone, although it's a Saturday and she should be with her family. Her sanctuary, always, has been the world of concept, theory, and logic. On tough days, she reclines on the couch in her darkened office behind a locked door, formulating new hypotheses and theorems, lulling herself into an alternate reality. And this is one of her toughest days, May 15, 2004, the anniversary of People's Park.

At dawn, the significance of the date found light as she struggled to wake up, drenched in sweat, running, nowhere to go. She could smell the tear gas again and see her father's face.

Brill, of course, had seen her, and just as she'd imagined, he was proud of his girl. He bragged about it to Lucy when she bailed him out of the city jail. At that moment, feeling a pang of mother's love, Lucy began to formulate her plan for the second and final escape to Ohio. They couldn't go immediately, had to let Verna finish out the school year, but the extra month gave Lucy time to work out the details. At all costs, they needed to get out. Away from Brill, away from Berkeley, away from that girl who was bringing Verna down. Indeed, Lucy had guessed enough to smell trouble, not too late, she hoped, to save her daughter.

This time, they settled in their own small house on the edge of nowhere. Ripped from what she'd known,

Verna was not in the mood to make new friends, and she turned again to books, immediately enrolling in summer courses at a junior college. For companionship, she clung to bb's fat letters, dwelling in a distorted dream of the past.

Come fall, as she wandered solitary through the halls of a new high school, she remained connected to her friend in the written word. Long distance telephone calls were never contemplated in those days, yet there was a belief in lasting friendship without voice or touch. Before long, Verna would return to Berkeley to see her father, maybe at Christmas, or if not then, no later than spring break, and bb would be waiting there, snug in their cocoon.

As the year wore on, the letters dwindled but never ceased as Verna was steadily drawn into the joy and comfort of her intellect. It became clear that junior year would be her last, and she sent off applications to colleges. She could not be interrupted in these academic pursuits for a visit to her father, who'd done little to maintain the lines of communication. The man who could fight for a park couldn't seem to fight for a daughter.

Lucy was the one, finally, to arrange a return. She had legal matters to attend to in Berkeley, but more important, she believed in the value of fatherhood and in Verna's need to see her father. She made plans for a summer trip to Berkeley, where they would stay with friends.

When she announced it, a mad excitement overtook Verna. It wasn't about her father. She was angry at him and didn't much care to see him or their old house where he still lived. The real attraction was bb.

Three weeks in advance, she sent off a letter and almost immediately started her daily run to the mailbox, looking for a response. During those days of waiting, she took an inventory of her stockpile of letters in the drawer where she'd saved every one, finding, to her surprise, that the most recent was a single page dated nearly two months ago. A bad feeling crept in and descended full force on the day she opened the mailbox to find her own letter returned, unopened and banged up, stamped "addressee unknown."

She did not believe in that smudged, purple-ink message applied by an ignorant postal clerk. She had to see for herself.

On a June afternoon, a year after their last hug on the cracked walkway, Verna took that path again up to the front door of the little house in the Berkeley flats. The bushes had grown bushier and the weeds taller, with a realtor's sign sprung up in their midst. The house was locked and empty. She knocked anyway, just to hear the confirmatory echo bouncing back. The occupants had disappeared without a trace.

The night before, in her old house, she'd been shocked to see Brill looking so changed with his unkempt, shoulder-length hair and eyes nearly gone to madness. But she didn't feel shock now as she stood in front of bb's empty house, and that meant there was something predictable in this situation. She was angry. Not at her friend—that would come later—but at herself for letting bb slip away.

In their year apart, with her head clear of forced

substances and false dogmas, the first iterations of Verna's essence had taken root. She'd discovered the beginnings of her adult person, her preference for lucidity, prudence, responsibility, and restraint. Tranquility could be eked from boredom, results from hard work.

In the methodical way she had about everything, she commenced a search during that week in Berkeley. Most people she asked were unaware that bb had left. A high school acquaintance had heard that the family moved to Oregon. Another thought that bb had run away, and the family had gone to look for her. There were rumors of bad trips and overdoses. The people who remembered anything realized they hadn't seen her since sometime in the spring. A secretary at the high school confirmed this. In mid-April, bb told her favorite teacher she'd be dropping out. The next day she was gone, leaving no forwarding address.

In the midst of these discoveries, Verna humored her mother with another uncomfortable visit with Brill. He smiled and bounced and exclaimed inappropriately. She didn't understand half the things he said. Something had snapped in him, and he would never be the same.

It was a relief to return to Ohio, where the search for bb continued from afar. Verna wrote to everyone she could think of. Fear controlled her actions, she couldn't deny it. Something bad might have happened.

But the world didn't stop because of it. She survived the rest of that summer when she turned seventeen, went to college and grad school, and lived the beginning and middle of the rest of her life. Time dissipated the fear, uncovering a belief in bb's continued sunny existence on this planet. And with that belief came the certainty of betrayal. The stark facts proved it. Between the two of them, only one had the ability, easily, to find the other, possessing knowledge of an address in California and an address in Ohio.

Thirty-four years later, all her searching for naught, Verna sits in a coffee shop in Boston, across the table from the newly materialized desaparecida. They are two women in middle age, each infinitely complex.

Verna's recent lectures swim in her mind. *In recursion, the function being defined is applied within its own definition, defining an infinite statement using finite components. In this process, components are repeated in a self-similar way.* If this is so, and if, when they were both sixteen, they discovered a common subset within each of them, experienced a natural convergence, a fated intersection, then why had they evolved in this way, spinning off into beings so utterly at opposite poles?

She can't fix the hideous dichotomy on exterior appearances alone because she and Isabella have meta-morphosed predictably, like time-lapse photography. The years are in their faces as they gaze upon each other again, the woman who was true, and the woman who was not.

Verna is thinking this way, knowing that something so crass would never enter the mind of the woman across from her. Isabella sits prettily unaware. Verna sits to judge the new betrayals she observes as they vie with that huge one from the past for her attention. There is the backup singing and the hair color and the biggest, most obvious betrayal, a protruding surgical alteration underneath

Isabella's clingy jersey. But the sexuality is packaged, controlled, synthetic, sunny, wholesome. She is what she was so many years ago, the blankness in the eyes removing her corporal self from the dirtiness and defilement of her surroundings.

And Verna knows what Isabella can see sitting across from her on the other side of the table. A dowdy, graying, bookish, owl-eyed professor, staid, respected, and ostensibly mature. Is the anger visible or as carefully hidden as she'd like to believe?

In mind-numbing avoidance, they continue where they left off, speaking around the edges of the glacier that sits on the table between them. They take turns reciting their respective CVs in broad outline, each leaving a glaring blank for 1970. Verna is acutely aware of the omission and assumes that Isabella is equally aware behind her glistening smile—has she had cosmetic dentistry?

Verna shows snapshots of her children.

"Oh, they're beautiful! Just like you. I'll bet you're a wonderful mother!"

"Well, I try. It *is* difficult these days. I worry about them, of course."

"I'm sure you do."

"Children must be protected. From so many things. Car accidents, violence in the schools…" She attempts to read something, anything, in Isabella's confident composure and celebrity smile. "…sex and drugs." Nothing.

"My goodness, what a challenge!"

The past cannot be provoked to the surface, and barrenness does not seem to concern Isabella, secure in her singleness and childlessness. But wait, what is this?

"You remember Tina?"

"Of course. Your little sister."

"She has two girls, a little younger than yours. Twelve and fourteen. They still live in California, in Concord. Here, look!" She pulls out a wallet with the school photos of the two nieces, and Verna can see the love in Isabella's eyes, the same love she saw that first afternoon in the kitchen, the big rush and hug and soaring emotion.

"They're beautiful," says Verna, feeling softer now, more open, allowing the next question to come without forethought. "How is Zenith doing?"

"Zenith?" Isabella has retracted into the void, staring back without responding, evoking sudden regret in Verna. Her own mother Lucy, at age seventy-five, is still a vibrant Ohio farm girl. Her father Brill, with whom she maintained a distant, intermittent relationship over the years, died in 1996, in a questionable, solo car accident.

"Sorry. It's been so long since she stopped using that name! My mom died two years ago."

"I'm sorry to hear that."

"Lung cancer."

"I'm sorry."

"Yes, I miss her."

It is the first point in their conversation when the eternal smile fades and a hint of deep sorrow emerges. The sorrow is completely healthy, a feeling evoked by the memory of a very close departed loved one, the kind of person who gave of herself during life and is guilty of no serious transgressions against the living. And it's the kind of sorrow that Verna cannot say she felt at the death of her own father. And it's the kind of sorrow that renews the anger she's temporarily forgotten and spurs the next question from her mouth, cruel and unthinking.

"How is your stepdad, Ray?"

Isabella squirms and slightly blanches. She looks down at her hands. This is a direct hit, but maybe it's the reason she's traveled the distance of space and time to appear in this coffee shop in Boston to face Verna, her sole witness.

"Ray." She gives that embarrassed little laugh from so many years ago when he unexpectedly entered her bedroom.

Verna remembers the glittering, dilated eyes, the finger wrapped in bb's curl.

"My mom left him, a year later."

Verna doesn't ask. It is the unspeakable year.

Isabella shakes her head, still looking down. "He wasn't a nice man." She speaks gently, in a controlled, schoolteacher voice, the sides of her mouth turned down. "No. He wasn't very nice. Not very nice at all."

The sterilized contempt is chilling.

Verna breaks into a sweat, her heart racing. A creeping dread rises from her gut, announcing her devastating mistake, the faulty moral judgment.

Isabella looks up, and what is this in her eyes? It presses through the studied blankness, a message surfacing from a finite component in the depth of her core.

You know what I'm talking about! Don't ask! Don't ask!

Verna won't ask, just as she didn't so many years ago.

She has an urge to run, but when the running is away from oneself, there's nowhere to go. "Excuse me," she says, pushing up from the table, overcome by vertigo. Just before she falls, the deep, sweet blackness rushes up to meet her.

⌇A SIMPLE CASE

ASSISTANT DISTRICT ATTORNEY Dana Hargrove had prepared her case well, as much as her tight schedule and the inevitable surprises allowed. Senior members of her bureau would have been amused had they taken a moment to notice her ardor, perhaps fondly remembering, but not admitting, their own enthusiasm from an earlier time.

She was an assembler of objective facts, whatever might lead her to the truth. Lies and things ignored or deliberately withheld only caused complications, and so she searched every set of events, every witness's statement, hungering for the crystal vision that life on city streets wouldn't yield.

Lofty ideals were rarely practical in the midst of chaos. At best, they simmered inside her conscience, perhaps too keenly felt, disturbing her preparations for trial. Only a year out of law school, class of '87, and nine months into the job, she was already unbearably overloaded, sharing a noisy office with three other rookies. The two metal file drawers reserved for her use were stuffed tight with misdemeanor cases, over two hundred

of them, all with her name on the outside: ADA
Hargrove.

In her profession, "garbage" was the generic term for
these cases, given to first-year assistants for wetting their
feet on the way to greater skill. Most of those slim manila
file folders contained no more than a couple of pages: the
complaint, the DA write-up, the defendant's yellow sheet.
Representing no more than a speck of city crime, her
cases nonetheless affected perhaps a thousand lives: the
cops, the defendants, the victims, their families and
friends. These faceless people vexed her soul, nettled her
curiosity, and aroused her sympathies in the way that
names and epitaphs on tombstones always did.

ADA Hargrove's first trial had begun as a prose-
cution against three defendants, now down to one after
two pled guilty. The defendants should have been
charged with burglary—a felony. But lacking any direct
evidence linking them to the break-in, the supervising
ADA in the complaint room had charged them with a
misdemeanor, criminal possession of stolen property. In
that way, the case had begun its bumpy descent down the
stairs of the system—a felony that became a misdemeanor that became "shit" (another term of art) after
the suppression hearing.

Hargrove saw it coming midway and kicked herself
later for not predicting it beforehand, wondering how she
could have expected something different from the
Honorable Brenda Johnson (known as "JJ" among
Dana's colleagues in the DA's office), a former Legal Aid
lawyer, veteran of the defense bar.

The ADA arrived in court for the hearing in her

best-pressed state, barely rumpled from her burden of carrying too many file folders and a fat law book from her tenth-floor office in the criminal courts building to the fifth-floor courtroom, AP-5, the "All Purpose" part. In the hallway, the defendant, Tyson Handler, skulked in a corner about six paces from his court-appointed attorney, Paul Cortina, who shifted from one foot to the other, empty handed except for the nub of a burning cigarette between two fingers.

"Tell me when the judge comes in," Cortina told the prosecutor with a blasé nod, his diamond earring flashing. Hargrove regarded him with a nervous smile, glancing at him long enough to register a complete mental picture: the aging sport jacket, crooked tie, and curly hair brushing the top of his collar. Her adversary earned about as much as she—somewhere in the low thirties—but displayed his poverty openly in a studied concoction of hair, clothing, and impudent swagger designed to characterize the underdog.

Hargrove pushed the swinging door of the court-room with her backside and stepped in. The courtroom was a small makeshift one, formerly an office for court clerks who had been unceremoniously shunted into a corner of the basement in the name of budget cuts and the burgeoning court docket. Sitting on the sole bench reserved for the audience was Police Officer Dave MacMarney, her witness for the hearing. Further in, near a side door, sat a court officer with his crossed legs propped up on a table, head bent over a curled paperback.

Stopping first to exchange a few words with her

witness, she went to the counsel table and plunked down her book and files. "Is the judge on her way?" she asked the court officer.

Without a blink he continued reading, as if he hadn't heard the question. But of course he had. A full ten seconds later he looked up and deigned to speak. "You know I can't call her until everyone's here and ready."

"The defendant and his attorney are in the hall."

"Okay. Why don't you go get them? If you want to start, that is."

She pursed her lips and glared at him for an instant, then averted her eyes, too embarrassed to engage in a stare-down with this man near the top of the seniority list, counting the days to retirement. Fuming her way to the swinging door, she poked her head out and called to Cortina, "He won't get the judge until you're in here." Cortina smiled. A sly smile, she thought.

Cortina stumped his cigarette in the ash can by the door and swiped the air with his head to motion his client inside. In no hurry, the two men shuffled in and assumed their positions at the defense table where, she noticed for the first time, Cortina had previously laid a slender file folder. Handler sat in the chair indicated by Cortina, the seat farthest from the jury box. The defendant was a small, wiry youth, noticeably unaccustomed to wearing a jacket and tie, looking as though he were mentally re-counting his attorney's instructions to sit tall and maintain a poker face.

The court officer made his promised phone call and within five minutes the side door opened. "All rise," he intoned. The black-robed judge strode toward the "bench"—a gnarled wooden desk elevated on a poorly-crafted riser—and nodded to the parties as she sat. "Let's get going," she said, all business. "What do you have Ms. Hargrove?"

"The People are ready for the suppression hearing."

"Well, call your witness."

The hearing was quickly underway, and halfway through the testimony, Hargrove's confidence began to build. It was, after all, a simple case, but every detail counted in proving a legal basis for admissibility of the key evidence: a small, round mantelpiece clock stolen from the burglarized apartment. Minutes after the crime, Officer MacMarney had recovered it from Handler's jacket pocket.

She was good at details, and details there were. Some of them were not very impressive—like the fact that her star witness was a rookie just like her, straight out of the police academy and on the beat for just six months. But she elicited Officer MacMarney's credentials with pride, then nailed down the facts of the arrest with precision.

MacMarney and partner, on patrol in a gentrified section of town at two in the morning, came upon three youths in their late teens: one at the wheel of a car, another loading a TV into the trunk, and defendant Handler nearby on the curb, standing next to stereo equipment. MacMarney alighted from his patrol car and asked what they were doing. The one loading the TV said they were "moving," while Handler glanced nervously about and placed his hand inside his sagging jacket pocket. Officer MacMarney quickly patted the outside of the pocket, felt something heavy, and retrieved the small clock. The car took off and Handler fled on foot with the suspect who'd been loading the TV. Officers apprehended them all, several blocks away.

Hargrove didn't miss a fact, and Cortina's sloppy cross gave her nothing to worry about. MacMarney was cool and honestly sure of himself. It was a question of self-protection. Any other officer in the same situation would want to know what was in that pocket before the suspect decided to use the object against him.

"But there was no outline of a gun?" asked JJ during Hargrove's legal argument, after the witness had left the stand.

"No, Your Honor, but…"

"Just a bulge."

"Yes, and other things…"

"A bulge is never enough."

"But the circumstances were suspicious, especially that comment about 'moving.' The officer was entitled to protect himself when the defendant made a furtive movement to his pocket."

"Furtive? Someone puts his hand in a pocket and that's furtive? Everyone has something in their pocket. This is a bulge case; you're just trying to dress it up with thin air. And don't forget, this defendant wasn't touching the TV. As far as your cop knew, he was taking a walk and happened to be next to the car." JJ paused before delivering the final blow. "I'm throwing this out. Motion to suppress granted."

Hargrove's eyes shot wide in disbelief. Judge Johnson was still a defense attorney, now disguised in judicial garb. The court officer sat up, more to stretch his back than to indicate his reaction to the proceedings, and resumed his indifferent slouch. The defendant and his attorney, both with forearms and laced fingers on their table, wore identical smirks. Cortina, who hadn't uttered a word of legal argument, was decidedly pleased that the court had made his job easy.

The judge impatiently banged the eraser end of a pencil on the desk, its even rhythm accompanied by the rattling of an antiquated air conditioner, while everyone in the room waited for the ADA's response.

"Well," said the judge at last, "are we going on? What else do you have?"

Hargrove, still standing in the aftermath of her legal argument, didn't speak immediately.

"I haven't much time for this. I'll give you two minutes to call your supervisor, or whatever you have to do." The judge whisked out the side door, her black robe ballooning behind her. Cortina stood and leaned intimately toward his adversary. "I'll be in the hall. Call me." Tyson followed his attorney out the door.

The young prosecutor finally sat down and stared blankly at her notes, faced with making a decision she hadn't anticipated. She could stop everything now and appeal the court's suppression order, get it overturned and then come back for trial, but that process would take a year. Minimum. The defendant was in court, now, miraculously present to preserve his $500 bail, perhaps his only money in the world. But JJ surely would return his bail money pending an appeal, and a year from now, with the evidence that much staler, Handler would be in the wind.

The alternative was to go ahead with the trial, but only if she had enough evidence to proceed. The clock was gone, but everything else established that Handler was an accomplice of the other two, helping them to get away with the stolen goods. Legally, it was enough to convict—she just had to convince a jury. Handler didn't deserve to walk out the door today: his yellow sheet had three prior arrests for stolen property, one dismissed, and two resulting in sentences counted in mere days. She knew what to do and would not be asking that paperback-nosed badge-shirt to let her use the rotary dial phone on his desk to call her supervisor.

"I'm ready," she told the court officer.

He looked up with that familiar insolence. "Hey, I'm happy for ya."

"I'll get Cortina and the defendant."

"You do that."

Judge Johnson appeared surprised to hear the news, but then, with the flame in her eye that had caused many juries to acquit in her time, immediately ordered a panel of jurors sent up for voir dire. Less than an hour later, six jurors and two alternates were selected and sworn, and after a lunch recess, testimony commenced.

The trial would be over in just a few hours. The victim of the burglary, a young woman, testified about finding her fire escape window broken, her apartment ransacked, and the TV, stereo equipment and mantelpiece clock taken. No, she did not see the burglars—she was nowhere near the apartment at the time. Officer MacMarney repeated his testimony for the benefit of the jury, careful, of course, to omit any reference to the mantelpiece clock in the defendant's pocket. Judge Johnson even prevented Hargrove from eliciting testimony about the telltale "bulge." At the close of the People's case, the defendant predictably declined to testify, and the defense launched into closing argument.

Cortina's strategy was not surprising. He had taken his cue from JJ's implausible suppositions during the hearing: his client had just been out for an airing and happened to be in the neighborhood of a burglary. "He wasn't with those two other guys, he wasn't helping them load the stolen goods, he wasn't touching a single piece of the property," whined Cortina as the young prosecutor bit her lip. JJ's suppression order implicitly authorized Cortina's argument, which, to Hargrove's ears, sounded more like a string of deliberate falsehoods.

During her own final argument, Hargrove implored the jurors to use their common sense, to ask themselves why the defendant would be out on that street at two in the morning, why he stood so near the other two youths and the stolen stereo set, why he ran with one of the other suspects when the officers came. A few heads nodded, but expressions remained blank or indifferently pleasant.

After the jury retired for deliberations, JJ turned to ADA Hargrove. "Don't go too far," she warned. "This is going to be a quick one."

Hargrove, Cortina, and Handler stepped out into the hallway, but almost immediately, they were called back in. The clerk delivered notes from the forewoman with questions the jurors must have blurted out to one another the second they set foot in the jury room. "What happened to the other two men?" "Was that small clock ever found?" The judge, in consultation with the attorneys, formulated answers that said, in so many words, "never mind" and "none of your business."

With these troubling questions out of the way, deliberations quickly concluded within another half an hour. The six jurors entered the courtroom, this time not in a file but in congenial, shifting pairs of smiling, relaxed faces, looking as if they were longtime bosom buddies at their high school reunion. ADA Hargrove knew what was behind those faces but wouldn't believe it until the words "not guilty" tripped easily from the forewoman's mouth as she cast a motherly smile in the defendant's direction.

Cortina immediately moved to seal the record—his most decisive and impressive act thus far—and the motion was granted. Judge Johnson turned to the jury with a beaming face. "Thank you, ladies and gentlemen. You have performed a valuable service. You are free to speak about the case or not, as you wish. You are excused with the court's thanks."

Feeling small but conspicuous, ADA Hargrove stood as soon as respectability allowed and said, "Thank you, Your Honor," a lump rising in her throat beneath the carefully assembled dignity in her expression. Defeat weighed heavily on her shoulders, much heavier than she ever expected it would, and doubt swelled where none had been felt before, adding a sense of self-disdain for the decisions she had made along the way.

She gathered her book and papers, all the carefully thought-out notes, and left the courtroom ahead of everyone else, then paused and lingered in the hallway.

She had no reason to flee and didn't want the others to think she was running.

Two jurors pushed out opposite sides of the swinging door and held it open for the remaining four. They were chatting and smiling, all of them now fast friends, these women and men who had met for the first time only hours ago. ADA Hargrove considered whether she should approach them to ask their impressions of the case and of her performance during the trial, but thought better of it and opened her face into a smile meant to convey her gratitude and her availability for comment. Each one in turn glanced in her direction, their relaxed and smiling faces one by one hardening into polite smiles for her benefit, their eyes darting away as soon as they'd lit, not wishing to linger with implicit invitation.

All six had turned away from her, continuing on their merry course toward the elevator, when one of them—the forewoman—paused and turned back, taking a step in Hargrove's direction. The others, sensing the absence of their leader, also turned and hovered uncertainly, wanting to overhear.

"There's just one thing I want to ask you," said the forewoman.

The prosecuting attorney brightened. "Anything at all, Mrs. Butler."

The older woman's polite smile had vanished, replaced with a haughty scowl. "Just where do you and your office get off prosecuting a boy like that?"

Hargrove felt numb and stared blankly.

"Just what gives you the right to charge someone with a crime for going on a walk at night? Can you tell me that?" Mrs. Butler's mouth twisted into a righteous smile accented by glowing eyes. The other five smiled or snickered in agreement.

Hargrove felt the urge to tell all, to divulge the evidence that had been kept from them, and to gain the upper hand once again, turning those sneers into remorse-filled apologies. But then she recalled a few things, important things. Little good would come of revealing that they'd been lied to, instilling a sense of betrayal in these conscientious citizens, the ones who hadn't dodged jury duty and had made a considered judgment based on the evidence they'd been given. Besides—she wasn't sure—but she probably had an ethical or legal obligation not to tell. After the acquittal, the court "sealed" the case, a fictional act of obliteration that prevented public viewing of the case file and any other record of the proceedings. The law existed to protect those who had been falsely accused, but its protections extended to all acquitted defendants, whether they were innocent or just lucky.

She mustered an even smile, intended to be steady and reassuring. "This case was prosecuted because I looked at all the facts and applied them to the law and made the judgment that there was enough evidence."

Mrs. Butler shook her head. "Facts? Where are the facts? Maybe you need a reality check. You know. Just get out in the streets and see what's going on instead of writing your theories down on a yellow pad."

"Maybe you're right, Mrs. Butler." Hargrove's eyes sparkled with levity, and a wry laugh escaped her lips. "Maybe I need a reality check."

The forewoman, with a self-satisfied air, hiked up her shoulder bag strap and turned to go.

"There's just one problem," said Hargrove.

Butler twisted her head back and raised her eyebrows.

"Reality. There's always more than one version to choose from."

The woman shook her head and walked away, her shoulders jerking in near-silent laughter. She joined her friends near the elevator bank.

Cortina and the defendant—no longer the defendant—pushed out the swinging doors. Handler had reverted to his leaning limp of the underworld and was talking fast and cool to his attorney. Cortina, with head lowered, muttered some final words to his client and shrugged him off by way of farewell, quick to put distance between them.

The lawyer approached Hargrove, coming up close enough for her to smell the stale smoke on his nervous breath. "You win some and lose some," he said, lighting up a cigarette. "Listen, the guy wasn't all bad. He's got a mother who loves him." He chuckled and took a long drag.

The red light flashed on over the elevator with an institutional sounding bell. One at a time, the six jurors shuffled inside, as Handler ran to catch it. He squeezed in beside Mrs. Butler, then held the door and craned his neck out toward Cortina.

"No, man, go ahead," said the lawyer with a wave of his hand. "Gotta watch my wallet," he said to Hargrove out the side of his mouth, chuckling again.

Stressed by the manual interruption, the elevator door remained frozen open for several seconds. Handler moved backward and sideways, closer to Mrs. Butler, flashing her a toothy smile. She responded with a pleasant smile of her own and faced front, elevator fashion. Handler eyed her obliquely, starting at the face, moving down to her earrings, necklace, strap of her shoulder bag, jacket—Mrs. Butler pulled the two sides together—down to her dangling pocketbook and diamond ring on the hand that clutched it.

With a grin, Handler turned to face forward as the elevator door closed slowly and shut hard with a final, metallic slam.

〰TO FLY

ONE NIGHT, I dreamt I was flying. My body, in a "t" shape, was floating freely with arms outstretched and legs straight behind, the sun on my back and a warm breeze ruffling my long hair. No flapping wings, just an easy, gentle glide. Far below were thickets of trees, a lumpy-soft quilt of green cut by twisting blue waterways.

The next night, I went to bed without a thought of that dream, but later, in the middle of a deep sleep, I remembered how wonderful it had been and I willed it to happen. "Dream the flying dream again," I told myself, and I did, easing effortlessly into the same "t" shape, hovering in the same timeless suspension, supported by caressing air currents. I flew for hours, never wanting to come down.

I haven't had a flying dream since. For many nights after the second dream, I repeated my internal somniloquy and gave the command, "Dream the flying dream again." But every morning I awoke with only a memory of the command, not the dream. Soon, even the commands stopped, as I surrendered to an evident powerlessness over my dreams.

* * *

I would come home from work and he would be sitting on the couch in the dark, watching TV, drinking beer.

"Any luck today?" The cheer in my voice took some effort. I spoke to his profile, cast in a blue-gray glow as he looked out at the world from backstage.

Things hadn't always been that way. Our daydream lasted a good couple of years, frozen in a memory of hazy bliss like a romantic photograph, misty around the edges. He was able to forget himself and what he assumed others expected of him. I received his undivided attention and soul-felt endearments, which meant more to me than material things.

There were a few gifts that seemed to come out of nowhere. One day he presented me with a gold and ruby necklace. He squirmed with anticipation and couldn't wait for even a second. "How do you like it?" he asked with a jaunty air.

I was startled to see the reckless thrill in his eyes. "It's beautiful," I said. "I love it, but…"

"Then put it on!" His tone was urgent with frantic joy. I swallowed the questions and met his demand, turning my back to him for help with the clasp. His fumbling assistance was followed by a proficient embrace and an hour of tumultuous lovemaking.

I actually believed—I still believe—he saved his money for months to buy that necklace. He was a working man to be sure. He would trudge off every morning at the same time for days in a row. These periods were followed by tense weeks when I saw little of him, after which he would resume his regular, daily trudging.

He spoke little of his work, giving me only a vague sense that a job existed and that his boss was a sonuvabitch who didn't appreciate him. I came to realize that the boss was a string of bosses at a series of menial jobs, each one the same in his eyes, each one beneath him.

I married him without a proposal after a period of hints and suggestions. Mine. We arrived late at the chapel, our two witnesses in tow. I couldn't tell you where these people are today.

Before stepping inside, I pulled at the skirt of my pink suit and adjusted a silly veiled hat I wasn't used to wearing, causing me to drop my bouquet. He picked it up and gave it to me with one hand, while tilting my chin up with the other. His fingers were moist and slightly tremulous. "Don't worry," he said earnestly, his face pale. "You're marrying the greatest guy in the world!" His eyes were at once fierce and dewy with love.

Even now, I can't remember the day it started, the change in his eyes. Slowly, one day at a time, the look crept in. I pretended not to see, but after a time, I came to understand it. My insight deceived me and wouldn't save me. The days were ticking off to that irreversible moment.

Early on, I came to dread social functions, especially those with my colleagues. Always that unavoidable question: "And what do you *do*?" On one occasion my husband was a college professor. On the next, a civil engineer, and the next, a tax accountant. His face was always a picture of affable sincerity. I would hang on a cliff waiting for that question and his answer to it, my fingernails pushing deep into the crumbling earth as I looked down, knowing I couldn't fly.

There were my decisions to remember, my mistakes to account for.

Afterward, alone with him, I would say, "It's not so terrible to tell the truth."

"I'm quitting that job anyway."

"Well, you could say, 'I'm looking for a job right now.' Everyone can relate to that."

This was the type of suggestion to make him turn away in disgust. "Always preaching. I only said those things to make you proud."

Other times were different. We would laugh and share outrageous could-have-saids. "Next time I'll say, 'I do what everyone else does. I eat and breathe. At night, I have my wife.'" His laugh was hearty, broad shoulders shaking. He was a big man, more than a head taller than me.

"How about something more philosophical? You could say, 'you're asking the wrong question. It doesn't matter what we *do* in life, it matters who we *are*.'"

"Who am I? I'm a man who doesn't *do* but is *done to* like 99 percent of all the men on this earth!" This time, his laugh came out skewed and bitter.

Soon we stopped socializing with outsiders altogether.

* * *

There've been many other days before this one, all my fault.

I confess my maddening habits, the neatness, the professional respectability, the enviable practice of bringing home a paycheck. He reacts. But there's been a glimmer of hope in each reaction, still time for a reversal. It didn't hurt. Not really. I can figure this out.

Each night I'm grounded, and each day I awake with the thought that this may be the one. This day.

I come home and find him in his usual spot on the living room couch, pulling on a can of beer. I can see him from the front door. He flinches when I close it, still staring straight ahead at the tube.

"Hello," I say softly, the way I always do now. He makes a kind of snorting sound before taking another gulp of beer.

The place is a mess. He needs to produce this evidence of his existence, or else he's goading me to say the one thing that will trip the wire. Either way, he isn't aware. I'm the one who's aware and can figure everything out.

I lay my stuff down on the hallway table and go into the kitchen to start dinner. I take some pans out of the cupboard in a normal way, I think, but the response from the other room is a couple of hits on the volume control, sending the manufactured drone of a newscaster to a deafening pitch.

Our dinner will be rice, green beans, and pork chops. He likes pork chops. Rice and water in a pan on the stove on high, beans in the steamer to turn on later, chops under the broiler. He'll like this dinner, part of the plan to save me.

It's a warm June evening. The kitchen is small and soon becomes uncomfortably hot. Propped against a countertop, my mind goes blank for the minute or two it takes the rice to boil. A mental vacuum, my only means of escape. The entrance to the kitchen is wide open with no door to separate it from the dining room, which leads to the front hallway and the living room on the other side, but I'm locked in, unable to move beyond a three-foot strip bordering the countertops and stove.

The rice starts to boil over—an inexcusable mistake that will leave sticky white crud around the burner. I turn down the flame, the white foam subsides, and the lid resumes its uneven steely "ping" on the edge of the pot. I open the broiler and grease pops under the flame, sending me a step backward—directly into his rigid stance. My heart leaps to my throat and I turn. "Oh!"

"A little jumpy?"

"No, you just startled me. I didn't hear you come in."

"When's dinner? You've been cooking for hours."

I glance through the glass door of the oven. "Soon. Only a couple of minutes. I…I can call you."

He stands inches away with arms folded, head and shoulders towering above. His mouth is set in a grimace and his eyes burn holes into mine, but they're not completely changed, not yet. Things could go either way.

I take a step backward, knowing I must be careful. Anything I say or don't say, or do or don't do, might precipitate the change. He remains planted, waiting, watching me check on the rice and turn on the flame under the beans. I've run out of things to check and know that I must say or do something. Standing still and mute will be an invitation. But I can't try to coddle him, or talk about anything inane like the weather, or say something to the other extreme—something personal enough to suggest the source of his pain. I decide on some words that seem innocuous enough.

"How did everything go today?"

Immediately I see my mistake.

"How did *everything* go?" His eyes are glittering, on the way to the change. He waits for my response, ready to jump on it. I still have a chance.

"Yes, just, I'm just asking how you are."

He laughs and steps closer. "No, you aren't."

"But—"

"You asked me how did everything *go* today. You think I'm stupid?"

"No, I just…"

"You're riding me again. 'How did everything go?' What do you think? Just great."

The beans start to boil and the meat sizzles and snaps under the broiler. Soon, another five minutes, it will start to burn. In the second before he speaks again I back into the counter for support, my eyes cast downward, hearing the sizzle and snap, praying that whatever he does won't last more than five minutes.

When I look up again, his eyes have made the change.

I step to the side, looking for a way around his impenetrable mass, but he blocks my way, ramming a hand against my shoulder.

"Where are you going? Tired of riding me? Sick of

getting on my case?" Bestial eyes, black and keen, rip into me. Those eyes hurtle against the glaring white of a padded cell. Those eyes are behind bars, frantically tripping between the slats. I can't look at him and drop my head low.

"Answer me!" He grabs my chin to force my head up, fingers like hot pokers. "Answer me!" slapping my face hard, making the room go black for an instant, making the tears roll. "Answer me, answer me!" over and over again, the sting of his hands on my face, sending me back against the refrigerator. The meat sizzles and pops, I lose my balance, knees hit the floor. He kicks me hard, "Answer me!" once, twice, shoe to ribs, no air to breathe, then a third time for good measure. For a second, nothing. I see the open doorway and make a run for it.

Everything is automatic, choreographed by an unseen puppeteer. I grab my purse from the hall table and bolt out the door. This time the car keys are inside, placed there earlier under direction of my inner voice. More than one time I ran outside without the keys and roamed the windy streets sweater-less, nowhere to go.

I've left the driver's side door unlocked. This is the day, after all. I jump into the car and hammer down the lock before he's on me, banging on the windows while I fumble with keys, drop them, pick them up and find the right one, jam it into the ignition. "You can't get away that easy! You can't!" His fists pound the glass so hard it shatters into fragments without breaking through. The next second I jerk away, bucking him off the car.

Two blocks down the street, I remember the oven. He won't let the place burn down, he's not that far gone.

But, as soon as I say it, I realize I no longer care.

After a safe distance I pull over to firm up my gelatin arms and legs. My face in the rearview mirror is white as a sheet, a drop of blood on my chin under a cracked lip. I massage my ribcage, feeling sore but not critical, knowing I'll heal from the bruises that will be visible tomorrow.

He could have done worse, he didn't have to let up. Proof of his love. I laugh out loud in the empty car, my sides hurting, cheeks wet with tears.

The evening is warm, so I open the convertible top of my aging coupe before turning the key in the ignition and setting out for the edge of town. The light blue of the sky is beginning to deepen with approaching twilight. Without a plan, I leave the buildings behind and take a winding road into the hills, remembering midway that I might be able to see a sunset from the top of the ridge overlooking the valley.

Ignoring the speedometer, I take the familiar curves fast, one after another around outcroppings of rock, maneuvering the wheel easily, letting the wind sing in my hair, turning my head casually to gaze out over the edge where the drop gets steeper the higher I climb. I'm nearing the top now, going up and up, not wanting to reach that dividing line where the descent begins. Pushing, extending the hill beyond its limits, I'm evaporating like the slow rise of steam into the atmosphere until I feel the slip of gravel under the wheels, a thrust over the edge into the open air, and the exhilarating surge of flight.

Below me spreads the green quilt, shaped by the

snaking waterway. I'm up here in the blue, dotted with white puffs of clouds turning pink around the edges, a sliver of orange sun on a distant horizon. A rush of fresh air fills my nostrils, my head reels with the thrill and I'm floating, just like before, everything quiet in suspended time.

This flight can't last forever, I know, but I've found what I need just in making it. On a gentle air current, I glide to the other side and touch down lightly, feeling the pavement solid beneath the turning wheels. I drive on and on through the sunset, into the night, believing in the certainty of my escape, never looking back.

∿BETWEEN BOYS AND MEN

MITZI'S HEAD STILL felt light and airy, and she couldn't help noticing her reflection in the store windows on the way to the subway. Yesterday, her hair had been cut again, this time to make the long side even with the short side and to remove the last bright blue ends from its natural light brown color. And now, everything else about her matched too. Her arms swung free and weightless with the colorful plastic bracelets instead of her metal spike armlets.

She stepped into the subway car and fit her petite frame into the remaining space on the bench. Her new, tight skirt obeyed her form well and felt nice where she sat. It was black (she hadn't quite broken the black habit), and short enough to expose her knees. She looked down at them, pale around the edges where they pressed against her normal pantyhose—not the black ones, or the white ones with the two-inch holes.

With knees pressed tightly together, she looked up to see five snarling faces in a poster labeled with big red letters. "CALL CRIME STOPPERS. N-O-C-R-I-M-E." Only one of them seemed to be looking at her: Darryl

Felder, age thirty-five, Caucasian, brown hair, blue eyes, 5'11", scar in left eyebrow. Wanted For Rape. For a moment, she was drawn to his face—a round face, not the expected lean, angular one—unshaved, with greasy strands of hair on his forehead.

She shuddered and lowered her eyes to the passengers across the aisle. They didn't seem to notice. As usual, they looked straight up or down or to the side, daring to glance at one another only when safe.

Mitzi giggled to think of the games she and Hawk used to play on the subway. They would pick out certain passengers—usually the most strait-laced business types—and make up bizarre, scandalous life stories that supposedly lurked behind their bored faces. Or, sometimes, they would just stare unblinkingly at their victims until they squirmed.

She and her boyfriend must have looked quite the pair: her jagged, blue head next to his vivid orange Mohawk.

All of that seemed so childish now that she and Hawk had been apart for two weeks. She'd told him it was over, she was looking for a "man" now and didn't want "practically an adolescent." It was 1987 and she was through with punk.

This feeling had come over her suddenly about a month ago on her twentieth birthday. Boys her age were simply too young. She cringed at their babyish vocal displays of attempted manhood. She became restless and irritated at the smallest things Hawk said or did. Honestly, she couldn't remember what it was about him that had attracted her. She supposed that the most he deserved was a place in the back of her mind where she stored all her fond memories: Hawk, her "childhood sweetheart" from those carefree high school days.

If only he would stop calling her, as if she hadn't meant what she'd said.

At her stop, Mitzi stood and made a tiny adjustment in her skirt before stepping off the train. Her new persona was delicate, poised, demure. She walked as best she could in this new self, trying hard not to wobble on her high heels. They were difficult to get used to after sandals and flats, but she was determined to wear them. One of her friends who worked as a receptionist in an office downtown always wore this kind of outfit to work, and besides, the shoes were very flattering. She confirmed this with another look in a full-length store window.

Fifteen minutes before opening time, Ramona, the store manager, was already at the art print shop, doing inventory. She glanced up absentmindedly to say hello to Mitzi, then looked a second time for a longer appraisal, tilting her head down to peer out over her funny half-size glasses. She smiled.

"Well, it looks like you've completed the new image."

Ramona really was "okay," so Mitzi didn't mind the comment. She hadn't quite figured out why she felt so comfortable around the conservative middle-aged woman, but she suspected it might have something to do with the fact that Ramona had even hired her in the first place. Six months ago, Ramona had been the only prospective employer who hadn't given Mitzi an incredulous look when she came to apply for a job.

"You like my hair?"

"Very much. It becomes you. What does Hawk think?"

"Oh, I haven't been seeing Hawk now for ages."

"Ah-ha," said Ramona, her expression enlightened. But sensing the delicacy of the subject, she turned to other things and explained what had to be done in the shop.

The store was small, and they worked alone together on weekdays. As usual for a Monday, the customers trickled in and out by ones and twos in between long minutes of emptiness. At about one o'clock, when Ramona was out to lunch, a man entered. Mitzi looked up from behind the counter, and their eyes met.

"Hello," he said, his eyes lingering on hers. Mitzi responded with a smile. The man was well-dressed in a gray business suit, his hair impeccably combed. His jaw was shaved so closely that it almost shone. He began to look at the posters displayed on the wall.

"Can I help you with anything?" Mitzi asked.

"I just thought I'd have a look. I'm moving into a bigger office today and need to brighten up the place with a picture or two."

He continued to scan the walls until his eyes fixed hard on a particular print, yet Mitzi felt included as a subject of his concentration. Without warning, he turned and threw his gaze like an angler casting a line in her direction, catching her eyes with a glint of steel gray in his. Just as abruptly he spoke, and the gray turned to baby blue.

"Is this a Paul Klee print?" he asked.

"Yes, you guessed it. 'Messenger of Autumn.'"

"I like it. I'm drawn to it. The colors are so subtle, except for that bright, orange oval that just captures one's attention. That must be the 'messenger.'" He chose his words carefully, spoke softly and rolled the language over his tongue, enunciating as though he were reading Shakespeare, all the while looking at Mitzi with glassy, interested eyes.

He decided to buy the picture, announcing his intention with a soft, deliberate command. As Mitzi walked out from behind the counter to retrieve the print, his eyes lowered, then quickly darted away from her legs.

"Actually, I'd like to have it framed. Do you have a copy already framed?"

"No, but I can have it framed in a few days. You'll have to leave a deposit though," she said apologetically, and returned to her fortress behind the counter.

"That will be fine, just fine. Put the entire amount on my card." He came very close to the other side of the counter and produced a credit card with the name "Darryl P. Fallon." The hand that pushed the card toward her was stark white with immaculately clean nails, filed and buffed.

Keeping her eyes averted, she asked how he might like it framed, then busied herself at the credit card machine to shake the feeling of his keen attention. He made no reply at first, then said it was best to leave the "artistic decisions" to a woman.

Mitzi finally dared to look in his eyes as she handed him the card, but just then the door opened with the tinkle of the bell. Her eyes jumped nervously toward Ramona, who entered with an assertive push of the door and a brief inspection of Mr. Fallon.

"Hello. Has Mitzi found what you were looking for?"

"Yes. Everything." He walked to the door, turned toward Mitzi to say that he would return on Friday, and uttered a polite "thank you" before leaving.

Ramona waited until he was thoroughly gone and asked, "Did that man give you any trouble?"

"No. None at all." Mitzi's pulse was racing and she felt excited but nervous to think that the man liked her; she could feel it. And such a mature man! She guessed he must be at least thirty-five or thirty-eight or something, but he was sending her all the signals, and in such a polite and restrained way, so manly and chivalrous and commanding, yet sensitive. In a way he seemed almost too polite and careful, but she supposed that her reaction to his manner was the result of her recent overexposure to impolite boys.

She looked at Ramona. "Wasn't he so...," she searched for the word, "distinguished?"

The older woman looked at the fresh young face with a peculiar, discouraging expression and replied, "I wouldn't say that."

Mitzi slammed the door and heard Lisa's groan from somewhere inside the apartment. Entering the living room, she saw Lisa sprawled everywhere on the floor—one leg stretched straight out to the side, the other, who knew where, buried under a pile of papers. Lisa sat with her back hunched over, squinting at small print in the dim light, her index finger twirling a lock of her bangs—the one that stuck straight out from her forehead during exam weeks.

"Why don't you ever turn on the lights?" Mitzi clicked on an extra lamp. "You'll ruin your eyes."

Lisa was sullen under her twirling finger. After a moment she said, "Why don't you tell that boyfriend of yours where to go?"

"He's not my boyfriend anymore."

"That's the problem. Maybe if he *was* your boyfriend he'd stop calling every five minutes. I swear, I'm gonna unplug that phone."

The telephone rang.

"Pick it up and tell him to go to hell. I have an exam tomorrow."

"I'm not talking to him." Mitzi retreated to her room but remained near the threshold.

The phone rang again and again, about fifteen times. Lisa picked it up. "Hello? *It's for you, Mitzi!*" she screamed and dropped the receiver.

Mitzi quickly reemerged and picked it up. "Hello," she said in her most impatient tone.

"Uh, hello, Mitzi?" He sounded mousy. Yes, he sounded exactly like a little mouse, she thought.

"Who else did you expect?"

"I've been calling you, I mean, for a long time. An hour. Aren't you late?"

"No, I'm not, and what's it to you anyway? You've got to stop calling. You're driving Lisa crazy."

"I just, you know, I just wanted to say hello. How are you doing?"

"*Fine.*"

"I heard, someone told me, like, you look completely different. Completely straight. I mean, they said you look real good and everything."

"Oh. So you have someone spying on me."

"No, no! Nothing like that. He just saw you on the street today. I think you probably were, like too far away to see him. It was Billy—you know—from the 'stute." Billy was another boy, one of Hawk's precious friends from the Art Institute, where Hawk pursued his fantasy of being an artist by producing mountains of drawings, mostly of subway cars, motorcycles, and broken beer bottles.

"Well, I guess you wouldn't understand that sometimes people just have to move on in the world."

"No, I mean, I think it's beautiful. Actually, I stopped shaving today, and I'm thinking, you know, I might cut the 'hawk when the sides get long enough. I mean, maybe I'll even grow all of it long, you know, 'cause a lot of people are getting back into this '60s look now."

"I'm very happy for you." Mitzi glanced down at Lisa, who gave her a dirty look. "I have to get off now. Lisa can't study."

"Okay. But why don't we, you know, let's get together sometime. I mean, at least we could be friends."

"Maybe. But look. Don't call anymore, all right?"

Mitzi hung up, went into her room and flopped down on her bed. What a child, that boy.

* * *

On Friday at 1:30, Ramona had already been back from lunch for ten minutes, but he still hadn't come. Mitzi, sitting on a high stool behind the counter, broke her stare at the front door to inspect the creases in her new purple synthetic leather miniskirt.

"Aren't you going to take your break, Mitzi?" Ramona spoke in her usual absentminded way, not looking up, masking her watchfulness.

"I guess so. I'll go now."

Mitzi picked up her matching purple drawstring purse and walked out, with the tinkle of the bell and Ramona's uplifted eyes behind her.

Down the block, she noticed Mr. Fallon coming toward the store, walking neatly, precisely, wearing a dark blue suit and red patterned tie. He was looking at her and kept looking with a slight grin on his lips as he approached and came very close.

"You're not leaving for the day already?" he asked without saying hello. He seemed to tower over Mitzi, the diminutive waif.

"No. I knew you were, well, I'm just going on my lunch break." Her face was hot and her high heels even less supportive than usual.

"In that case, why don't I treat you to lunch?" The question was a soft command, making her uneasy but in awe of his manner—so understated and polite.

"Sure, that would be nice."

He seemed pleased: his eyes flashed a sharp gleam, like a silvery knife's edge in the sunlight. "Good. I know just the place."

They walked, and he didn't touch her or say where

they were going, but she felt guided and didn't stray from his path, although her vision was impaired as if she were blindfolded with a gauzy cloth. She couldn't think of much to say, but he didn't seem to mind.

They stopped, and she turned to him before he had the chance to completely remove his downcast eyes from her body.

"Is this the place?" she asked.

"This way," he said, and led her down into a basement that suddenly became an elegant restaurant with dark wood paneling and thick, white linen tablecloths.

Several heads turned as they were escorted to a table in the corner. The waiter pulled out a chair and she lowered herself insecurely, relieved to feel the seat underneath when she sat. Mr. Fallon immediately started to survey the wine list, while Mitzi began to worry about whether their lunch would be finished in her allotted hour.

"Wine?" he asked. But before she answered, the waiter was there to take his order for a five-year-old chardonnay. With a slight bow, the servant whisked off on his silent mission.

Mitzi glanced around her. The other men and women looked like lawyers or bankers in their expensive business attire. She started to think of Hawk's laugh and how he would make things easier and funny if he were here, but she quickly pushed the thought away. With Hawk it had always been Dutch treat at a fast-food restaurant. She'd risen so far above that.

"So, how do you like the place?"

"It's very nice," she said with amazement, then

corrected her tone: "I pass by here a lot and was thinking of stopping in for lunch sometime."

His lips formed a small, polite smile, and he extended an open palm to indicate the leather-covered menu before her. She studied it with care, trying not to show her concern at the indecipherable French.

Shortly, the waiter appeared with the wine in a silver bucket. Mr. Fallon nodded his head when the bottle was displayed and accepted the glass with a sample. He expertly swirled, sniffed, and tasted the wine—glancing up at Mitzi once or twice in the process—and gestured his approval to the waiter, who filled their glasses. The pouring done, the waiter stood obediently at attention nearby.

Mitzi had decided on the selection that seemed the least difficult to pronounce when Mr. Fallon suggested that she try the "pool" something, which was "prepared exceptionally well here." He rattled off a string of French words in a flawless accent, and the waiter again disappeared.

Having survived these initial ordeals, Mitzi immediately came to miss the comfort of the waiter's presence. Conversation was not forthcoming from Mr. Fallon, whose eyes consumed her as he slowly sipped his wine. She did not question his entitlement and felt shyly flattered to receive such steady attention until, out of the blue, an image popped into her head—Ramona's disapproving eyes peering out over her glasses.

Mitzi took a sip of wine and made an attempt at conversation. "So, I guess you must work around here too?"

He lifted his chin and looked down at her along the slant of his nose. "Just like a woman," he said, with an edge to his deliberately polite tone of voice. He paused, as though he expected her to know what he meant, then explained: "Always wanting to find out immediately what a man does for a living!" His mouth emitted an abrupt, snorting laugh, and Mitzi giggled to show that she understood his point.

"I'm in business," he continued.

"What kind?"

"Manufacturing." He appeared satisfied with this answer and made no attempt to offer more.

Mitzi nodded knowingly and remarked that his business "must be very exciting," adding, "I plan to get into the business area myself." Having difficulty finding the correct words, she explained her ambition to start night courses in typing and "receptionist work" at the Grace Worth Business School once she had saved enough money.

"Very admirable for a girl in your position. I do think that some women are exceptionally well suited for the business world while others are more suited for the home," he said, dwelling on the word "business" even longer than the rest of his carefully chosen words.

She fairly beamed at this expression of approval. He lifted his glass and said, "To your future career in the world of business." Their eyes locked as she clinked her glass against his and took another sip of the wine, feeling its effect already racing to her head, straight from her empty stomach.

Time no longer seemed to matter as Mitzi's head

became fuzzier. She tested her newfound courage and ventured to look at him for longer and longer moments. His immaculate appearance impressed her—the smoothness of his face, the purity of his white shirt, the symmetry of his tie. Almost nothing was out of place, except an inexplicable sheen on his upper lip despite the pleasant temperature of the room.

When their lunch arrived, she was pleased to see an attractive arrangement of chicken in a smooth sauce next to colorful vegetables. The food was the best she had ever tasted, and half of it was gone before she remembered to cut off petite morsels.

Mr. Fallon refilled their glasses and asked if she lived alone in the city.

"Yes, I have my own place. I mean, I don't live at home. I'm sharing an apartment with someone."

He raised an eyebrow. "I see. Another girl your age?"

"Yes. She's a student."

"Ah. Two women of the world then."

Mitzi didn't quite understand this sophisticated-sounding comment. "I guess so. But it'll be nicer when I don't have to have a roommate."

They lapsed into another interval of silence invested with eye contact—his nearly continuous, hers occasional. During their attempts at conversation, he revealed little about himself and spoke for more than a sentence or two only when talking about a subject in an abstract, philo-sophical way. As she was describing her work at the art print shop, he launched into a speech about the "importance of art and beauty in one's life," his lips caressing each word as they formed it.

Mitzi, not quite sure how much she had drunk, was surprised to see the empty bottle at the end of the meal. The check came hidden in a little leather book which Mr. Fallon opened and signed, then gave to the waiter without money or a credit card. Fortunately, the waiter again helped Mitzi with her chair, and she gathered herself foggily.

Outside, the sunlight was excessively bright. Mr. Fallon started to go, but she reminded him that his print had been framed and was ready to be picked up. He apologized, explained that he had a meeting to attend, and said he would return on Monday. He came very close without touching her, said goodbye, then turned and walked away quickly.

Mitzi looked at the clock as she entered the shop. Only twenty minutes late—amazingly. She walked behind the counter and deposited her purse.

"Have a nice lunch?" Ramona asked in a tone that said she was aware of the time.

"Yes. I'm sorry I'm late, but I saw Mr. Fallon outside and he invited me to lunch."

Ramona was tugging on a sticky storage drawer, trying to open it. "Who's Mr. Fallon?"

"The man who was here a few days ago. He bought that Paul Klee print we just framed. He'll be back on Monday to pick it up."

"Ah, yes." Ramona winced as the drawer opened with a jolt, causing her to stumble backward. "Why didn't he pick it up today?" She wiped a bit of perspiration from her forehead and smoothed her graying hair.

"He was busy. He had a meeting."

Ramona considered this for a moment and said, "Hawk called while you were gone. He left a number."

"Oh—I told him never to call me at work."

"There's no problem with it, Mitzi." Ramona pulled out a wholesale book of art prints and started to leaf through the pages, her eyes cast down through the half-size glasses. "What do you think of that man?"

"Hawk?"

"No. Mr. Fallon."

"He's really nice and polite, but kind of quiet. He took me to an expensive restaurant."

"I see," Ramona said slowly, still looking at the book. "I think you should call Hawk immediately. He sounded very anxious to talk to you." She shot a quick look at Mitzi over the rims of her glasses. Unable to defy her employer's suggestion, Mitzi went to the phone in the back room, hoping Ramona might not be able to overhear.

"I have to see you," was the first thing he said, no longer sounding like a mouse but like a larger, wounded animal.

"I told you not to call me, especially not here!" Mitzi screamed at him in a whisper.

"Listen, why don't we go to dinner tonight and talk about it? I'll treat."

"What, hamburgers? No thank you. I don't want to see you—and stop calling!"

"Just let me come by tonight after…"

Mitzi hung up.

* * *

At the end of the day, Ramona had to leave an hour before closing time, and she asked Mitzi to finish up. She'd been doing this more frequently of late, especially on Friday nights, now that she trusted Mitzi with heavier responsibilities.

For most of the hour the store was hopping until, suddenly, Mitzi found herself alone. Fifteen minutes remained. She decided to take advantage of her luck and close early, hoping to avoid Hawk. Ever since his call that afternoon, she'd been worried he might show up at her scheduled quitting time, like he always used to do.

She turned the bolt lock in the front door, removed the cash drawer from the register and took it into the back room, where she flicked the switch to turn off the lights in the main room. She needed to account for the cash in the drawer and put it in the safe.

It was already dark outside and the streetlights had come on, casting long shadows along the dark walls where the framed prints hung. Only the small area where she worked remained illuminated. She never liked the feeling of being closed in and preferred to leave the door to the back room open. It was better that way, even though she felt somewhat on display in her tiny well-lit corner, as though anyone on the street could stand at the front window and look through the darkened shop to where she sat.

All was quiet except the hum of the fluorescent lamp above her and an occasional horn blast or shout in the distance from the street. She counted the cash—slowly, meticulously—and compared the amount to the sum on the paper receipt roll.

A sound. She jumped. Someone was knocking on the glass pane of the front door.

Hawk already! He's early, she thought. But she peered out and saw that maybe it wasn't him. The dark figure standing outside was much too large. The round circle of his head eclipsed the beam from a streetlight, leaving his face obscure with strange rays sprouting from his outline. She walked through the main room toward the door and saw that it was Mr. Fallon.

"You're not closed already?" His voice sounded muffled through the door.

Mitzi stood with her hand on the bolt lock and twisted back to look at the money lying on the table in the light. She scolded herself for having such a ridiculous reflex. Of course he wasn't interested in the money. She looked at him again. It seemed like years since they'd been together in the restaurant. The only remnant was her slight headache from the wine.

"May I...?" He motioned. She hesitated but could think of no reason to deny him entry. She unlocked the bolt and opened the door just wide enough to let him in.

"You're not here alone are you?" He looked over her shoulder, into the back room.

"My boss had to leave early. Actually, she left only a minute ago." Mitzi felt nervous and tried to think of a way to get to the light switch without revealing her unease. "I thought you were going to come by on Monday."

He didn't answer immediately but looked at her for what seemed a long time, his face shadowy in the nearly dark room. "This was the most convenient time," he stated and smiled with gleaming eyes. "Do you have my print?"

"Yes, I'll get it." She walked across the room and behind the counter, where she'd left the framed print, wrapped in brown paper. She turned and was startled to see him right behind her. They had moved into the fluorescent light emanating from the back room, but his face still looked shadowy, as if unshaved.

She bent down to pick up the parcel. Abruptly, he touched her shoulder. "No, let me." He picked up the package and carefully, slowly, placed it on the counter, as if it contained the most delicate crystal. He stroked the brown paper wrapping with the palm of his hand and lifted his eyes to meet hers. She was glued to her spot, only a few feet away from him.

"Well," he said at last, "do I owe you anything?" He continued to stroke the paper while staring into her eyes. She could almost feel the pressure of his hand. "I think I've paid for it," he added.

"Yes, completely. The credit card—you charged it." Mesmerized, she couldn't look away. The light was catching his face in an odd way, and there was something different about it, something she hadn't noticed before. Was it...? A small white spot that kept appearing in his left eyebrow when he turned a certain way. But a moment later, it was gone.

He stepped toward her, and a greasy strand of hair fell onto his forehead. He was very close. "You're sure you'll be all right here, by yourself?" She could feel and hear his breathing. He smelled of alcohol—but hadn't they drunk the wine a long time ago? It seemed like such a long, long time ago.

"Maybe," he said in a breathy voice, "you could use some company." A slow grin lifted the corners of his lips. "It must be quiet in here, all alone. I'm sure you'd like me to…" He took her bare forearm with a sweaty hand. She jumped back, but he held tight.

Her mind buzzed in a panic. Of course. *This* was the thing she should have expected. Still, she couldn't seem to move. His free hand was now between them, reaching for her face…

The bell on the front door tinkled. "Mitzi, are you still here?" She turned to see Hawk's silhouette in the doorway, the beam from the streetlight outlining the fuzzy half-inch stubble of growth all over his head.

Mr. Fallon dropped her arm and turned to look.

"Say, what…?" said Hawk.

Clearing his throat, Mr. Fallon picked up his package. He quickly maneuvered around the counter and walked toward the door, lifting his purchase an inch or two by way of explanation as he passed Hawk in the doorway. He took to the street in long strides and was gone.

"*Who* was *that*?" Hawk screeched in his adolescent voice. Such a familiar, comforting sound! Yet she couldn't respond. Her eyes were fixed on a point behind him, in the ghost Mr. Fallon had left behind.

Hawk came up to Mitzi and touched her shoulder. "Hey, you're shaking! What happened?"

For another moment, she couldn't move or speak. Hawk stood firm and tall, ready to protect, and like a man, he held back and waited for her. Finally, she draped her arms around his neck, pressed her cheek against his soft, baby-boy face, and found her voice.

"I guess I'm glad to see you," she whispered in his ear.

———————

Dear Reader

As I write the afterword to this updated edition, I'm celebrating a few book birthdays.

A little more than a decade ago, I gathered up all the stories I had written in the '90s and the '00s and arranged them in three volumes by theme: *Everyone But Us, tales of women*, *Dust of the Universe, tales of family*, and *Malocclusion, tales of misdemeanor*. Since the publication of these collections in 2012-2013, many readers have let me know how much they've enjoyed my stories.

During the same decade, I've published six novels of legal suspense in the Dana Hargrove series. (Dana was introduced to the world in the story "A Simple Case"!) Each one is a standalone, finding Dana at a discrete stage of her family life and career. If you enjoy courtroom drama, legal thrillers, mystery, and police procedurals, these novels may be for you, starting with the first one, *Thursday's List*. The sixth, *Power Blind*, releases in January 2022.

Let me know your impressions of my stories by posting a reader review of any length with your online book retailer. You can also drop me a line through the contact page on my website, vskemanis.com, and I'll respond directly. The contact page also has a link to a free e-book offer.

To keep up with the latest on my books and life, find me on Goodreads, YouTube, BookBub, Facebook, Twitter, and Instagram, and subscribe to the blog on my website.

Thanks for reading!

V.S.K.

January 2022

Opus Nine Books

All works published by Opus Nine Books are dedicated to the nine members of the family headed by John and Kate Swackhamer at 3 South Trail, Orinda, California—a large world under one small roof.